"I'm wondering if the gang might take on my husband's case."

"Your husband?" Lott asked.

"He was killed here in Las Vegas in May of 1992," she said. "Never solved. His name was Stan Rocha."

It was as if she had punched him in the gut. The Rocha case had been his first case as a homicide detective. He remembered clearly there had been no leads, nothing. Not solving that case had really set him back mentally early in his career.

She leaned forward, staring at him with a puzzled look. "You know the case?"

"I do," he said. "Are you sure you want this opened again?" he asked, looking at the worry on her beautiful face. "You know how cold cases can sometimes dig up things often far better left buried."

She nodded. "He and I were basically separated when he was killed. No real marriage left, not that there ever was one. But not knowing who killed him has eaten at me for twenty-two years now."

"I know that feeling," he said.

She frowned.

"Your husband's case was my first case as a homicide detective."

"Oh," was all she said.

ALSO BY DEAN WESLEY SMITH

COLD POKER GANG MYSTERIES:

Kill Game

Cold Call

Calling Dead

Bad Beat

Dead Hand

Freezeout

Ace High

Burn Card

Heads Up

Ring Game

Bottom Pair

DOC HILL THRILLERS:

Dead Money

"The Road Back"

KILL GAME

A Cold Poker Gang Mystery

DEAN WESLEY SMITH

wmg
PUBLISHING

Kill Game

Copyright © 2021 by Dean Wesley Smith

All rights reserved

First published in a different form in *Smith's Monthly* #6, March, 2014
Published by WMG Publishing
Cover and Layout copyright © 2021 by WMG Publishing
Cover design by Allyson Longueira/WMG Publishing
Cover art copyright © Fergregory/Depositphotos
ISBN-13: 978-1-56146-486-9
ISBN-10: 1-56146-486-4

KILL GAME

Kill Game:

Sometimes, in a fixed limit poker game, a kill hand is triggered when a player wins two hands in a row. The bets double at that point for the next hand. Kill Games up the risk and bet levels in a low-risk game.

PART ONE

CHAPTER ONE

May, 1992
Downtown Las Vegas, Nevada

The idea Jim had on a warm early-summer evening was to find the rumored place for afterhours dancing called "The Path." Jim had just graduated high school, the proud class of 1992. He was headed next year to Stanford, full academic ride, and he was really looking forward to getting out of the desert in a couple months. He had been born and raised here and was excited about living somewhere else. Anywhere, actually.

Jim stood barely five-nine, had long brown hair, and a moustache he was doing his best to grow and mostly failing.

Sharon, his girlfriend over the last six months, also now graduated, wasn't happy he was going so far away. She had been offered a scholarship at UNLV and had taken it. So between them there was a tension of the coming split.

Sharon was actually taller than Jim, with long blonde hair and skinny legs that seemed to always be stuffed into jeans a size too small. She had also done some light modeling and as she aged, she just got better looking.

Jim had no idea what she saw in him, but they always had such a good time together. They had two hobbies: Dancing and having sex in every place they could imagine or risk.

Tonight they were thinking of doing both at the same time. They had heard how really crowded the dance floor at "The Path" could be. Sharon had suggested, with a smile, that it might be fun to try a little "fooling around" on the floor while dancing.

Jim was game if she was. With Sharon, he would try just about anything. Logic often never played a part.

So they parked down on Paradise Road, about two blocks from the club, and headed down the sidewalk along the row of low warehouses, holding hands and laughing, the coming separation only a distant thing to ignore on such a wonderful spring night.

The club had an entrance off an alley into a large warehouse, but until two days ago, on Sharon's birthday, both of them hadn't been eighteen and old enough to get in, so they hadn't tried to find it.

Paradise had street lights and even though the area felt rough, both of them were native to the city and knew this really wasn't a bad area. They were as safe as they could be at midnight in Las Vegas.

Cars lined the street on both sides, so they knew they were in the right area even though they didn't know exactly where the club was. And between traffic on the street, if they listened hard, they could hear the pounding beat of the music echoing through the one-story buildings of the area.

"Maybe it's down here?" Sharon asked, pulling Jim into the first alley they came to.

Jim could tell at once they were in the wrong place.

4

And then the smell hit them.

The putrid smell of something rotting in the heat. It was a cloying smell that seemed to make the air thicker than it actually was, and fill every sense. It turned his stomach instantly. He knew it was a dead person instantly. He had smelled that before. He had no idea how police who worked around dead bodies ever got used to the smell.

"What is that?" Sharon asked, stopping and covering her mouth and nose. After a moment she started to back toward the street, her eyes round and her skin pale.

Jim stood his ground. He had been with two friends last year up on Lake Mead when they found a floater near the shore. He knew that smell. Someone had died.

But there was no body in the alley. Just walls of warehouses. Not even garbage cans.

He stepped toward one wall and the smell decreased.

"Jim, get out of there," Sharon said from the sidewalk behind him.

He motioned to her that he would be right there, then stepped toward the other wall. Originally a white stucco wall, it was now stained with years of grime and lack of paint that he could see even in the dark shadows.

And the smell got much worse.

There was no door in the wall, just a nearby high window that was cracked slightly.

Someone was dead in that room beyond that window.

He turned and went back to Sharon, taking her hand. They went around to the front of the building, took down the address, then said, "We have a phone call to make."

He could see a pay phone a block away on the outside wall of a closed grocery store, so he started off in that direction.

"I thought we were going dancing?" Sharon asked, scrambling along in her high heels, working to keep up with his fast strides.

"We are," he said. "But we have to call the police first."

"Why?" she asked.

"That smell," he said.

"You are going to report a smell to the police?" she asked. "It was bad, but not a criminal offense I'm sure."

"I wouldn't be so sure of that," Jim said, letting go of her hand as they reached the phone and he started digging into his pocket for change.

"What do you mean?" Sharon asked, looking worried. There was one thing he really liked about Sharon. She was smart and knew he was smart, so they trusted each other on a lot of things.

"I've smelled that smell before," he said, as he dropped the coin into the phone and pushed zero for operator."

He glanced back at her puzzled expression.

"Near the body I found up at Lake Mead."

She put her hand over her mouth and even in the strange lights of the street, he could see she had lost most of her tan very suddenly.

The operator answered and he was connected to the police. He gave them his name, his location, and the address of the building.

Then he said clearly, "I want to report a dead body."

CHAPTER TWO

September, 2014
Pleasant Hills
Las Vegas, Nevada

Retired Detective Bayard Lott had just arrived home from the grocery store when the doorbell rang. It actually startled him, the high, ding-dong sound. It had to be someone trying to sell something, since no one he knew ever rang that doorbell. He didn't even know the stupid thing still worked.

He had his arms full of paper sacks of snacks and soft drinks for the evening's poker game. Plus a tub of Kentucky Fried Chicken he planned on having for dinner and to snack on the next few days as well. It smelled wonderful and made his mouth water as it filled the kitchen with promise.

He loved KFC. Never seemed to grow tired of it. A couple of his friends had said he was going to turn into a giant chicken leg if he wasn't careful and didn't balance the KFC with something green.

He only ever shrugged at that. As a detective, he'd seen worse.

It felt good to be inside in the cool air out of the heat of the early evening. It had to still be over a hundred degrees outside, far too warm for the middle of September. The fall cooling hadn't really started yet. Even being in an air-conditioned store and car, just getting between places was hot.

He dropped the supplies for the game and the chicken on the counter near the sink. The Cold Poker Gang met every Tuesday night downstairs in his basement poker room. He lived for Tuesday nights, he had to admit.

Usually there were four or five playing, all retired Las Vegas detectives. They got together, played cards, told stories about whatever, and worked on cold cases for the city.

At sixty-three, he felt he still had a lot to give to police work and solving cold cases made him feel useful again. He liked that.

All the members of the Cold Poker Gang did. And he enjoyed the poker games as well.

And KFC.

Didn't get any better than a poker game with friends and KFC. His version of heaven.

The doorbell rang again.

"Yeah, coming," he muttered to himself. "Not buying anything anyhow."

He made sure none of the sacks would tip off the counter and glanced at the clock on the stove. It was still a good hour before the game started. His best friend and former partner, Andor Williams was the only one who ever came early. He knew it wasn't Andor because his old partner never rang a doorbell. It seemed to be against his religion, if he had one. He liked pounding his fist on doors for some reason.

Lott headed out of his kitchen and across the formal dining area and then the front room. His wife, Carol, had died three years before, and the living room looked like she was still here, sitting in her big recliner, watching the nightly news.

He hadn't really touched a thing in that room. It had been her favorite room in the house and now he hired someone to keep it clean, but mostly stayed in the kitchen and the basement and watched television downstairs in his remodeled gaming room.

Trying to watch television in the living room just got him thinking of Carol too much and he did enough of that as it was.

Damn he missed her.

As he headed for the front door, he ran a hand through his still-thick gray hair and made sure his badge and gun were close by on the end table near the door.

He opened the door and was surprised to see retired detective Julia Rogers standing there, a Yankee's baseball cap pulled down over her light brown hair to shade her face. She wore her standard tan slacks and white blouse under a light dress jacket. At first glance she looked like a middle-management worker on her way home from work. But the baseball cap didn't fit that image at all.

Rogers had joined the game two months before on the recommendation of his daughter, Annie. He liked Rogers a lot. More than he wanted to admit to himself at times. He found himself thinking of her out of the blue.

But Carol had only been gone for three years and he just didn't feel ready to have another relationship, even though Annie was at him all the time to get out more and relax.

Annie had been the one to suggest he remodel the basement game room a year ago to make it all his. She was worried about him banging around in the house all alone with only the memories of her mother.

He understood that worry, but he still missed Carol every minute of every day. Nothing he could do about that. Carol was gone, he knew that. He was doing his best to move on with life. That was one reason he liked the Cold Poker Gang games so much.

Rogers actually had been a detective in Reno and had retired after having a bone in her leg shattered by a gunshot in a firefight with some drug dealers. She now walked with a slight limp that was hardly noticeable. She was only in her mid-fifties and had moved to Las Vegas to get to warmer weather and to play poker. From what Annie had told him, she was a good tournament player and had won her share of tournaments around town.

Rogers had bright green eyes that didn't seem to miss much and her sense of humor often kept all of them laughing. She seemed to have no trouble at all being the only woman in the Cold Poker Gang.

"Sorry to come early, Lott," she said, smiling as he opened the door to let her into the coolness.

He could tell her smile really didn't reach her eyes. Something was really bothering her.

"No problem. You can help me with the snacks and drinks."

"Love to," she said.

She followed him back into the kitchen where he grabbed a cold bottle of water from the fridge and handed it to her as she pulled off her baseball cap and shook out her long hair. Usually she kept it tied back, but for some reason today she hadn't done that.

Compared to his six-foot frame, she was almost tiny at five-two. But he had no doubt she was the toughest five-two you would ever want to meet in a fight. And he and Andor had taken her to the gun range off Las Vegas Boulevard and she was a better shot than both of them.

"Wow, that smells good," she said, indicating the chicken as he worked at the sacks, suddenly feeling very odd. Besides Annie, Rogers was the first woman who had been in the kitchen since Carol died. He glanced around, actually looking at the room.

He or Annie or the housekeeper had put away most of Carol's things from the kitchen, leaving it just kind of bare. Standard white appliances, gray stone counters, and a big stone-topped dining table with six chairs around it.

His cleaning service kept the kitchen cleaned and sparkling. But he seldom cooked much of a meal in it. And the fridge was full of take-out leftovers, usually boxes of KFC.

"The chicken does smell good, doesn't it?" he said. "You hungry?"

"I could use a piece. What can I do to help?" she asked as he unloaded sacks of chips onto the counter near the stove, plus a large bag of Peanut M&Ms for Ben "The Sarge" Carson. Sarge loved the things, but he often left most of a bowl full behind. Lott couldn't keep away from them no matter how hard he tried. So every week Lott had to buy another large bag.

"How about just sitting there at the table, work on a piece of chicken, and tell me what's bothering you?"

He slid the bucket of chicken over onto the table, then dug out some napkins and plates.

She laughed. "That obvious, huh?"

"I think the hour early sort of gave you away," he said, smiling at her.

"What?" she asked, smiling back at him with a grin he could

really come to enjoy. "Can't a friend just come to talk with another friend without there being something wrong?"

"Of course," he said, shaking his head and going back to unloading the sacks of chips and pretzels. "But that's not the case this time."

"Got me on that one, detective," she said as she dug into the bucket and put a chicken breast on her plate, licking her fingers off after touching it.

Then she sat there in silence until he joined her at the table and took a leg and thigh for his plate. The smell was heavenly and he had half the leg gone before he glanced up at her.

"Not sure how to say this," she said.

"Quickly usually works for me," he said, "Like pulling a bad tooth."

She shook her head and laughed. "That's one way of thinking about all this." Then she looked him right in the eyes.

He sort of jerked. She really was better looking than he had thought and those intense green eyes seemed to just look through him. He had noticed her a lot over the last two months and had even admitted to his daughter that he enjoyed the games even more since Rogers had joined them. But until now he had never been alone with her and really looked at her.

Clearly there was a connection between them.

"I'm wondering," she said. Then stopped again and looked down at the bottle of water in her hands and the chicken on her plate.

"Wondering what?" he asked, not really pushing. Just trying to help her get it out. He kept working on his chicken, giving her time.

She again looked him directly in the eye. "I'm wondering if the gang might take on my husband's case."

"Your husband?" He finished off the leg and then wiped his

hands. He had no idea about her past, but he had a hunch he was going to find out a lot more fairly quickly. And that idea actually excited him. He suddenly wanted to know a lot more about the beautiful woman sitting across his kitchen table from him.

"He was killed here in Las Vegas in May of 1992," she said. "Never solved."

That surprised him more than he wanted to admit. "What was his name? I don't remember a Rogers in the cold case files and I had just gotten my shield in 1992."

"Rogers is my maiden name. His name was Stan Rocha."

It was as if she had punched him in the gut. He pushed back slightly from the table. The chicken he had eaten suddenly seemed like a lump in his throat.

The Rocha case had been his first case as a homicide detective. He remembered clearly there had been no leads, nothing. Not solving that case had really set him back mentally early in his career.

She leaned forward, staring at him with a puzzled look. "You know the case?"

She must have been able to read his reaction as easily as he read her discomfort with coming here early for something.

"I do," he said. "Let's call Andor and get him over here early and see what he says. He's the one that gets the files from the Chief of Detectives each week."

She nodded and sat back.

"Are you sure you want this opened again?" he asked, looking at the worry on her beautiful face. "You know how cold cases can sometimes dig up things often far better left buried."

She nodded. "He and I were basically separated when he was killed. No real marriage left, not that there ever was one.

But not knowing who killed him has eaten at me for twenty-two years now."

"I know that feeling," he said.

She frowned.

"Your husband's case was my first case as a homicide detective."

"Oh," was all she said.

CHAPTER THREE

September, 2014
Pleasant Hills
Las Vegas, Nevada

Julia was stunned at how attracted she was to Lott. Over the years, since her husband's death, she had dated a few times, and even had one relationship that lasted for a few years. But mostly the relationship part of her life had been shut off for a long time. She had just assumed it would always remain that way. There just weren't a lot of men looking for fifty-some-year-old retired police detectives with a limp.

And until she had been shot and then retired and moved to Las Vegas to be near her daughter, she hadn't noticed that she missed having a man in her life. But now, for some reason, since joining the Cold Poker Gang, she had been attracted to retired detective Lott.

More than she wanted to admit.

He had a calm way about him, and seemed frighteningly

smart. She had even caught herself a few times looking at his wonderful head of thick, gray hair.

His daughter, Annie Lott, was one of the best poker players in the world and her boyfriend, Doc Hill, was pretty much acclaimed to be the best. Julia had met and liked them at a few tournaments, and sat next to Annie at one tournament for a few hours. When Annie, who also used to be a Las Vegas detective, learned that Julia was a retired detective, she told her about her father and the Cold Poker Gang. It had sounded wonderful and it had turned out to be even better than Julia had imagined it might.

Julia looked forward to Tuesday night now. Fun poker, fantastic company, and so far she had been involved in solving two cold cases, which had given her intense satisfaction, something she hadn't felt as an active detective in Reno for years.

And she loved the banter between the detectives, just like she had never left her department. She hadn't realized how much she missed talking with people who were blunt, funny, and trying to solve bad things that had happened to people. The gunshot wound had given her an out, but many times she wondered if she should have taken it.

Now she needed to have some answers as to what happened to Stan. And if the gang would take on the case, she might actually get the answers, good or bad, and feel like finally she could move on with her life.

They sat in Lott's kitchen, eating the wonderful-smelling KFC chicken and talking while waiting for Andor. They went from talking about the late-season heat wave to what Annie and Doc had done this summer up in the Idaho Wilderness.

"They keep wanting me to go with them once," Lott said, shaking his head.

"Sounds like fun to me," she said. And it did. Four days

rafting in wilderness area down the River of No Return seemed so distant from poker tables and murders, she loved the idea and had promised Annie she would try it next summer.

"Oh, no, you too?" Lott asked, shaking his head.

"The forces are pushing you toward the river," Julia said, laughing.

"The force is that daughter of mine."

"She is a force," Julia said, laughing and wiping off her hands after a second piece of chicken. She didn't realize just how hungry she had been.

"How come no more kids?" she asked, "If that's not being too personal."

"Not at all," Lott said, laughing. "Carol often joked I was more married to the job than her."

"I know that feeling." She loved his laugh and his grin. He was a very handsome man who clearly had loved his late wife.

She had loved Stan as well, but they just weren't making it when he was killed. In fact, their entire marriage had seemed just off somehow. He had seldom been around and when he was he seemed always too willing to please her.

She really hadn't wanted a passive, dull man for a husband. She had always imagined herself with someone strong, able to stand up for himself, and someone who could make her laugh.

A loud banging echoed through the house, making her jump.

"What the hell is that?" she asked, glancing around.

"It's either an earthquake or Andor," Lott said, shaking his head and standing, indicating she should just stay put. "I'm betting on Andor. He's allergic to doorbells."

She laughed as Lott went to the door of the kitchen and shouted, "It's open."

A moment later she heard the front door open and then slam close.

"I smell chicken," Andor said as he came toward the kitchen.

"We left you some," Lott said, sitting back down and smiling at her.

He came in and nodded to her. "Rogers."

"Andor," she said, nodding back.

That tended to be most of their conversations except over a poker table. She liked Andor a lot. She had known other detectives like him. Outwardly like a bull in a china shop, but inside very kind and generous and smart.

He headed over to the fridge, took out a bottle of water, grabbed a plate and napkin and joined them at the big table. Clearly he was used to being in this house and making himself at home. She had never gotten that close to any of her partners in Reno.

She envied that.

Andor's wife had also died a number of years before and from what she had discovered, his entire focus was now solving cold cases. He seemed to have no other life at all that she knew of. She at least played poker and had lunch with her busy daughter Jane once every week or so. When Jane had time to squeeze her in, that was.

He grabbed a couple of pieces of chicken on his plate and started into it, pulling the skin off with his fingers and eating it with two hands, one sliver at a time like a giant vulture picking apart a carcass. He never picked up the piece from his plate.

She and Lott both watched him for a moment before Lott smiled at her and she laughed.

"He eats like that with everything," Lott said, shaking his head. "I've watched it now for a couple decades."

"Yeah, yeah," Andor said, still working at the chicken piece, his hands covered in grease. "Why the rush-over-early call?"

Julia was glad that Lott took the lead when he asked his former partner. "Remember the Stan Rocha case?"

Andor snorted. "That thing we could never solve? Drove us both nuts. Why?"

"Meet the widow," Lott said, pointing toward her.

That froze Andor with a sliver of chicken halfway to his mouth. He looked at her intensely.

Finally he asked, "Joke?"

"No joke," she said, staring into his dark, intense eyes. "Rogers is my maiden name. I never took his. We were separated and not getting along much when he was killed."

Andor dropped the sliver of chicken and wiped off his hands, then his mouth, shaking his head the entire time.

"Let me guess," he said. "You think the gang should open the case?"

"I do," she said.

Andor again just shook his head, then looked over at Lott. "And what do you think?"

"I think it's about damn time we clear that case. It drove us both crazy for a year."

"And you think now is going to be any different?" Andor asked.

"No," Lott said, smiling. "But now we have the time and we have family help." He indicated her and she smiled at Andor.

"You two are nuts," Andor said, shaking his head as he dug back into the second piece of chicken on his plate. "But I'll ask the Captain next week."

"Thanks," Julia said, suddenly both excited and scared to death.

She needed to know what had happened to her husband.

But at the same time she wasn't sure she really wanted to know. She wasn't sure Jane wanted to know either what had happened to her father.

But Julia had a hunch that, as good as the Cold Poker Gang was at digging into cold cases, she was going to find out no matter what, now that she had started this ball rolling.

CHAPTER FOUR

September, 2014
Pleasant Hills
Las Vegas, Nevada

Andor showed up early the following week before the gang was set to arrive. Lott had been in the kitchen getting a glass of iced tea. The summer heat still hadn't broken and even though it was only a week from the end of September, the temperature had gone past one hundred yet again. He normally didn't mind the heat, but this summer it had started early and was lasting longer and he would be glad when the cool nights were back.

Andor banged on the door and Lott shouted for him to come in.

By the time Lott had the pitcher of iced tea back in the fridge, Andor tossed a brown file folder on the kitchen table and went for a bottle of water.

"The Rocha case?" Lott asked, taking his tea and moving over to the table. The folder looked really thin, far thinner than he remembered it. And had a coffee-cup stain on one side. Somehow his memory had built this case into a huge investigation. It hadn't been.

The folder had the standard "Copy" stamped on the outside.

"That's it," Andor said, taking his bottle of water and joining him at the table. "I left out the murder scene pictures of the body. No point. Let's hope Rogers can add some details because that case is as cold as they come."

Lott sat across from Andor and opened the folder, letting the memories of the early case in his career flood back over him. Over twenty-some years as a detective, he had had a couple-dozen murder cases go cold on him. But this had been his first case as a detective. Period.

And Andor's first case to go cold.

So they both remembered it clearly.

Male vic by the name of Stan Rocha, three shots, killed execution style, two in the chest, one in the head, at close range with a twenty-two. Body left in an empty warehouse off of Paradise Boulevard to rot. No way to trace the bullets, no shells left behind.

A couple kids smelled the body and called the police. The guy had been dead for a week.

Some mining company owned the warehouse, but were not using it for anything. The doors were all unlocked. No prints worth dealing with.

The case was cold almost from moment one. And that fact had driven them both nuts.

There was a notation in the file that his wife was a cop. They were separated, no issues, and that she was a cop in Reno and had been on duty all week. Andor had called and her chief vouched for that and they had ruled out Rogers as a suspect almost instantly and hadn't even bothered to interview her, since she sent them a report on what she knew of her husband's travels, which wasn't much.

And Rocha had no other family that they could find, or that his widow knew about. And she had no idea what he was doing in Vegas. She had thought he was in San Francisco looking for work.

Lott looked at the last page of the file. Neither one of them had even put a hunch of who they thought might be a suspect.

There were no suspects.

Lott closed the file and sighed. He felt as hopeless now on this thing as he had back twenty-two years ago. He hated that feeling, almost more than anything else.

Andor just shook his head. "This one is going nowhere quick."

"We'll see what Rogers has to add," Lott said, sliding the file back to his partner. "She might have picked up some details after twenty years."

"I wouldn't count on it," Andor said. "From what she wrote in that report she sent. Looks to me this Rocha pissed off the wrong people and paid the price."

"Doing what?" Lott asked. He pulled the file back to him and opened it again to make sure his memory was right. "Says here he had no drugs on him or in his bloodstream. And only twenty-two bucks in his wallet."

Again Lott closed the file. The Cold Poker Gang had tried a number of cases like this one over the last year. No leads, nothing. And those cases, for the most part, were still sitting on his bar downstairs next to the poker table. Why did he have a hunch this one was going to join that pile quickly, even with Rogers' help.

They didn't come any colder than this case.

"So what do we do first?" Andor asked.

"Interview the widow after the game tonight," Lott said. "Show her the file, see if something clicks."

Andor shook his head. "I'll leave that one up to you, partner. I got a date with eight hours sleep after we're done tonight. Last damn thing I want to do is dream about the Rocha case."

Lott nodded and just stared at the thin folder.

There just wasn't much there. And twenty-two years in the past was a long time.

CHAPTER FIVE

September, 2014
Bellagio Hotel and Casino
Las Vegas, Nevada

After the game ended in Lott's basement at about ten, Lott had told her that he had wanted to interview her and brainstorm about the case. But he said he didn't feel right doing that in his own kitchen. Something about the fact that he had never done anything like that in the past kept him from wanting to do that now. He had told her that he and Andor and other detectives over the years had sat at that kitchen table and talked about cases a great deal. But actually doing a sort-of interview in the kitchen didn't seem right.

So he had suggested to her that they go down to the Cafe Bellagio to get something to eat.

She had agreed at once. She told him she liked the place, since it had nice booths and comfortable tables and chairs, mostly surrounded by plants. It was always open. She had eaten many a meal there while playing in poker tournaments.

They took separate cars to the casino and when she arrived, he was already being seated in a booth that looked out at the entrance and had more than enough privacy.

"You know all the cop short cuts?" she asked, laughing as she slid in across from him.

"That and I use valet parking," he said, giving her that grin she was starting to really like, more than she really wanted to admit. He had a strong chiseled chin, intense dark eyes, and a sense of humor she was just starting to see. He was fantastically handsome for a man of any age.

"That's cheating," she said.

"More money than the desire to walk in this heat very far."

"Yeah, there is that," she said. "This is my first fall down here. Does it ever cool down?"

"Eventually," he said. "At least I remember it does, but you know how old cop memories can be?"

"No, how?"

"Shot to shit," he said.

She groaned as the waiter handed them both menus and took their drink orders. Even though it was after ten in the evening, they both ordered iced tea. Clearly he was a late night person as she was. She liked that.

After they both had ordered—him a BLT and her a chicken salad—he turned to her.

"Are you sure about opening this? Got to ask."

She had asked herself that same question a dozen times over the last month and that many at least since last week. She needed to know what had happened, if that was even possible. And from the look of the thin file they had on the murder, they were all starting from scratch decades late.

And she really, really appreciated that he was worried about her feelings on this. Made her like him even more.

"I am," she said, nodding like she really was sure. "Let's do this. Fire away, detective."

Lott reached down and picked a lined yellow legal pad off the seat beside him and slid it to her. Then he put another in front of himself. "We don't trust only one of us to write everything down. We're going to find the answer in the details and we both need to figure out those details."

"Worried about our old memories, huh?" she said.

"That, and just making sure we miss nothing."

She nodded and pulled the legal pad in front of her. He slid her a pen so she wouldn't have to dig one out of her small purse.

She was relieved beyond words that he was organized on this, at least this much. The murder of her husband had been so much of a part of her life that she had put away, she had no idea how to organize any of this.

"Let me start," he said.

"Please," she said. "Thanks."

"Do you have any idea as to his family background?"

"Nothing," she said. "He didn't much like to talk about anything in his past and in the four years we were together and married, it never once came up. We eloped, so no one but us was even at the wedding."

"So you don't know anything about his mother or father or family?" Lott asked.

"Nothing," she said, feeling amazed that was still her answer after all these years. When he died, she half expected someone to contact her from his family, but no one ever did.

"That's where we start," Lott said.

"I agree," she said. "That's bothered me right from his death."

She wrote "Family???" at the top of her blank page and felt a lot better.

Then she had a thought while staring at that word. She looked up at Lott. "Maybe someone missed him at one point or another?"

"You mean if he disappeared, someone might have filed a missing person's report?" Lott asked, frowning at her.

"Exactly," she said. "He was in Reno on business when we met in May of 1988. We were married three months later. I sort of bullied him into it, I think. He traveled a lot during those marriage years, always on business of some sort or another. I think it had something to do with construction because he often came in dirty, like he had been on a construction site."

"So you thinking we look at missing person's reports from 1988?" Lott asked. "I like that." He went to writing.

She did the same thing.

"And not only 1988," she said, wondering why she hadn't thought to check earlier, "maybe he never told his family about me and when he was killed in 1992, they filed a report then."

"Well," Lott said, writing as she went to write her thoughts down as well. "That's going to keep us busy."

"Easier now than in 1992," she said. "But chances are it will be a dead end."

"At least it's a path," he said. "We don't have many good ones at the moment with this case."

"Boy, don't I know that," she said.

They were served their late-night dinners and after the waiter left, she decided to confess something to Lott.

"Promise you won't laugh?" she asked as she picked at her salad.

"None of this seems to be funny to me," he said, then took a bite of a fry that came with his sandwich.

"I never even knew exactly what his job was," she said softly. "Married for just short of four years and I didn't know what he did to make money. And after he was killed, no employer contacted me."

"Did he have money?" Lott asked.

She shook her head slowly. "This is the embarrassing part. I found out after he died he was taking my money. A little bit here, a little there. Even though he said he was supposedly making a living and putting money into our account, it seemed I was supporting us both."

"You have money besides your police salary?" Lott asked, his food forgotten.

"Not a dime," she said, just about as embarrassed as she had ever felt in her adult life. "He moved into my small apartment with me and he had his own car. I just never noticed because he seemed to be employed. But after he died I discovered all our money came from me."

"Con artist," Lott said. He grabbed his pen and marked it down on his paper.

"But there was nothing he could con me out of except living expenses," she said. "I wasn't even a detective yet and never talked about my job at home. I never brought files home, and he never asked."

"You got all his belongings still?" Lott asked.

"Tossed his clothes, but everything else I have still. Two file boxes is all."

"We need to go through that," Lott said. "You, me, and Andor."

She nodded and went to work on her salad.

"You were young and you had no way of knowing," Lott said.

She looked up into his smile. It made her feel a lot better

that someone like him actually understood. She had never told anyone that information until now. Not even her daughter. She had tried to protect her daughter as much as possible from information about her father, what little information there was.

"Thanks," she said.

"So how long was he normally gone?" Lott asked.

"Sometimes up to two weeks or more at a time," she said. "Then he'd be back for three or four days, working at something around Reno, and then gone again. I was so busy being a cop, I hardly noticed, sadly."

"And you didn't pay for his travel?"

She had to laugh. "On my cop's salary?"

"So what was he doing?" Lott asked, writing on his pad as she wrote the same question on her pad.

"And where did he get the money for the travel?" she asked, adding the question to her pad as well.

Lott smiled and put his pad beside him, off the table. "Seems to me we have a lot of places to start."

"It does, doesn't it?"

She also put her pad beside her and for the next hour enjoyed a good meal and the great company.

If somehow she could put the death of Stan behind her, she might actually be able to really get on with her life. And having help doing that from someone as handsome as Lott was making her feel better by the moment.

CHAPTER SIX

September, 2014
Pleasant Hills
Las Vegas, Nevada

The heat seemed to be breaking a little the next day when Rogers showed up at Lott's place about two minutes before Andor. Lott had really, really enjoyed their late dinner last night and had promised her a chicken lunch the next day, straight from the nearest KFC.

He had gone out about noon and gotten that, since she and Andor were both due at one. The chicken now smelled wonderful sitting on his kitchen table. He already had the paper plates out and a bunch of napkins.

Somehow, he had refrained from taking a piece early, but his rumbling stomach had told him a few times that he should do just that. There was just something about KFC that could do that to him.

This time Rogers knocked loudly instead of ringing the doorbell. When he opened the front door, she was standing there with two old brown file boxes stacked in her arms, smiling over the top one at him like a kid over a wall. The boxes were the reason for their lunch. They were going to look through Stan Rocha's last possessions.

She looked like she was dressed to go to work as a detective again. Her long brown hair was pulled back and she had on a white blouse under a light brown dress jacket and brown slacks.

He could feel a slight jolt as he saw her again. He was going to have to watch himself. He really was falling for her. He wasn't sure, honestly, what he thought about that.

He had no doubt his daughter Annie would be overjoyed.

And he had a hunch that Carol would be saying "It's about time." Right before the cancer had finally taken her, she had made him promise he would move on with his life. He had promised, but not believed the promise. Without Carol, there honestly had seemed like no life to move on with.

But now, after three years, he realized just how smart his wife had been.

He held the door for Rogers and then took one box off the top as she passed him.

"Thanks," she said as she headed for the kitchen and he followed.

"Wow, that smells fantastic," she said. "Amazing how KFC uses that smell to sell chicken. I'm hungry."

"Me too," he said. "Haven't had much since the Bellagio."

She smiled at him as she set the box on the counter. "That was fun."

"It was," he said. "And productive. This morning, on the way to KFC, I came up with one more thing to add to the list. What had happened to Rocha's car?"

She jerked and then shook her head. "Never once thought of that either. I sure didn't get it. Damn, I really needed to pay more attention back when this happened."

"You were stunned he was dead," Lott said.

"Yeah, I had a lot of things going on. But I sure wasn't much of a detective on my own husband's murder."

"Were you a detective yet?"

She laughed. "Not for another three years."

"Well, I was," Lott said, "And it never occurred to me to wonder about a car. We just assumed he was killed somewhere we couldn't find and taken there."

"He might have been," she said.

"You remember the make and model number?"

"I do," she said.

He slid the second box next to hers on the counter. "You have the registration in these boxes by any chance?"

"Nope," she said, shaking her head, clearly stunned that she had never once thought of her husband's car. "I would have noticed it and that would have reminded me."

At that moment, Andor banged on the door.

"Grab yourself a bottle of water. Or there's iced tea in the fridge," Lott said, turning for the living room again.

"You want some tea?" she asked.

"Love some," he said over his shoulder.

He reached the small dining area and shouted across the living room, "It's open."

Andor came in, banging the front door closed behind him just as he always did. Lott loved Andor, but at times he moved through life like a bull in a china shop, not really caring what got in his way or what he broke.

"I'm starving," he said as he headed across the living room.

"I got the big bucket," Lott said, shaking his head and turning back into the kitchen.

"Perfect," Andor said.

When Lott got back into the kitchen, Rogers was pouring them both glasses of iced tea from the glass pitcher he had filled earlier.

As they sat down and dug into the chicken and corn-on-the-cob side that Lott had added, he filled Andor in on what he and Rogers had come up with last night.

"So let me get this straight," Andor said after licking off his fingers from finishing his first piece. "We search for his family. We search missing persons from around the time of his death, give or take. We look through this stuff here, which is his personal information he left with you, and try to figure out what he was doing for money. And we search for what happened to his car. Right?"

"Got it," Lott said, nodding.

"Well," Andor said, shaking his head and smiling. "That's about a thousand more leads than I thought we would come up with in this case."

Then he turned and looked directly at Rogers. "What kind of car was he driving and you remember where it was registered?"

"1989 dark-green Grand Caravan van. He seemed to carry stuff in the back of his van that he kept covered, but I wasn't sure for what. Always assumed it was for his job. Nevada plates on the van. No clue from what part of the state. I never once rode in it."

"Did you two have a joint checking account?" Lott asked as he wrote down all that information on his note pad.

"No," she said, shaking her head and looking at the half-eaten chicken leg on her plate. "But I know he had a checking account because he carried a checkbook. But he left no records at my place."

Then she stopped and realized what she had just said. "Damn it all to hell! I never thought to check for that either."

Lott watched her as she shook her head in disgust at herself and marked down that note on the note pad as well. He did the same on his note pad. Sometimes there were records of abandoned money and accounts, but he wasn't sure if they could find any accounts or if they did if the accounts would show anything of value. But it was worth looking into. Maybe he could get his daughter Annie to help on that. She and Doc, her boyfriend, had resources to do that sort of thing.

"And you have no idea what your husband did for a living?" Andor asked.

"Besides something in construction because he often came home dirty, basically he lived off of me," she said. "I discovered that after his death. He stayed in my apartment after we were married and I sometimes cooked. But I have no idea how he paid for all his traveling, or where he went all those weeks he was gone."

As Lott ate another piece of the luscious chicken, she went on to explain to Andor the same details about the marriage and what she had discovered after her husband had died. And the realization that she knew little or nothing about the man she married.

"He was a very passive guy," she said. "Now that I think about it, it's hard to imagine he made anyone angry enough to kill him."

"Doesn't take anger sometimes," Andor said.

"Yeah," Rogers said. "Then what?"

No answer to that one.

Lott knew that nothing about any of this was adding up

anymore than it did in 1992. But at least now they had something they could do, some things to trace down.

That was a start.

And a starting point was a lot better than they had had twenty-two years ago.

CHAPTER SEVEN

September, 2014
Pleasant Hills
Las Vegas, Nevada

After they finished the chicken and corn lunch, Lott cleared off the big kitchen table and moved the first box over. The light from the afternoon sun streaming through the kitchen windows was filling the room with clear light, and the overhead light filled in even more. It was a bright and comfortable place to sort things. Over the years, he and Andor had done just that at this table numbers of times, usually making Carol disgusted at some of the things they had to sort.

But she had been amazingly supportive. He had asked her why she didn't mind them doing things like that at her kitchen table and she had said simply, "At least you're home."

As a detective, he understood that. She had mostly raised Annie with him just being in and out. Amazing Annie had followed him into police work after that sort of upbringing.

As Lott dropped the first box on the table, Andor looked inside and then dumped it out on the table, spreading out the folders and a couple pens and a few small notebooks.

Lott took out his yellow legal notepad and across the table Rogers did the same, frowning at the stuff on the table as if she hadn't seen it before. More than likely it had been decades since she had looked at it.

Lott picked up one of the spiral notebooks and opened it. Nothing. Totally empty from front to back.

"Where was all this stuff?" he asked Rogers.

"Stan kept a small desk in the apartment, plus some of this stuff was in his part of the closet and in his chest of drawers. I put receipts and stuff in the folders as I found them in his clothes pockets and such."

Andor nodded and picked up one folder.

Lott waved the notebook. "Empty." He dropped it back into the box.

Rogers slid him another notebook and it was empty as well. In the meantime, Andor was sorting receipts looking for anything that might give them a lead.

"How are you sorting?" Lott asked as Andor started two piles.

"One for Reno, one for out of the Reno area."

"Good idea," Rogers said, taking another folder full of receipts and starting into them.

Lott did the same with yet another folder, sometimes finding it hard to figure out even a name on some of the faded bits of paper. As detectives, they were used to this kind of work and used to doing it carefully. It always felt to him like a combination of doing a puzzle and a treasure hunt. Sometimes pieces fit, sometimes they found the one treasure that would lead them to solving the case.

For an hour they worked mostly in silence, getting through both boxes, sorting out pens and a couple of empty keychains with names outside of Reno on them, plus all receipts.

Then when they had all the Reno paperwork pulled and all items that were Reno-based back in one of the boxes sitting beside the table, they looked at the remaining piles in front of all of them.

"I got Boise receipts," Andor said, "Salt Lake receipts, Winnemucca receipts, and Las Vegas receipts."

"The same in this pile," Rogers said, indicating the one in front of her.

"Exactly the same with mine," Lott said, getting a little excited at the prospect of actually seeing Rocha's life have a pattern. "So we sort by city."

They went back to work and after another half hour had four piles of receipts from out of Reno filling the middle of the table.

"I had no idea he traveled this much and this far afield from Reno," Rogers said, shaking her head. "I sure wasn't much of a wife not knowing what her own husband was doing."

Andor laughed. "I doubt this had anything to do with you. My gut sense is telling me your husband had a con going of some sort and that's what got him killed."

Lott nodded. He agreed with his partner, even though the idea of that clearly hadn't made Rogers happy. He couldn't imagine how she was feeling discovering this, even after all these years.

They spent the next hour sorting through and getting a general timeline on the receipts for each town. It seems that over the years he went from one town to the other like he had a route.

Lott made out a timeline on his notepad of the general times

39

Rocha had been in each city. It seemed, in general, his stays never seemed to last for more than three or four days at a time, usually once every three weeks. Just as Rogers had said was his pattern in Reno.

Then they focused on the Vegas papers since they knew the most about Vegas. Food receipts, gas, and so on.

"What's missing here?" Andor said after all three of them looked through the hundred pieces of paper from Vegas.

Roger shook her head, but Lott saw it almost at once when Andor asked the question.

"No hotel," Lott said. "Where was he staying during all this time here in Vegas over all these years?"

"Oh," Rogers said. "I'll be go to hell. Where was he staying?"

"These cover summers, winters, year-round for a number of years," Andor said. "He couldn't live in his car during the summers."

"And there were no other hotels that I saw in any of the other places either," Lott said.

"So who was he staying with?" Rogers asked. "In all of these places. No hotel receipts at all. None."

"We figure that out," Andor said, "and we might have our first lead."

"What the hell were you doing, Stan?" Rogers asked, staring at the piles of paper on the tabletop, as if they would give her an answer.

And Lott knew that eventually they might.

CHAPTER EIGHT

September, 2014
Boulder Highway
Las Vegas, Nevada

After they got done sorting receipts on Lott's kitchen table, they planned their attack on the case.

Julia was stunned at how much she had already learned about her ex-husband. It had never occurred to her to sort those receipts like that. Or even look through them. After she got the news of his murder, she had just boxed up everything and tossed the two boxes in the top of a closet.

A couple of weeks after that she had sold his desk and given his clothes to The Salvation Army. She had just cleaned him from her life and gone back to work and having his baby. She still wasn't sure why she needed this solved now. Part of it was because she was attracted to Lott. She knew that.

And part of her knew she could never really be in another

good relationship until this was cleaned up. Or at least until she made an attempt to clean it up.

But it was amazing how much more she now knew about her former husband than she knew when married to him. That just made her sad that her one and only marriage had been such a sham. What did that say about her?

After sorting the receipts, their plan was pretty simple. Andor was going to head downtown to the police station and see if he could get some searches running for missing persons in the Boise and Salt Lake areas, using Stan's picture and the make of his car. And see if the car was impounded back in 1992 somewhere here in Vegas.

The impound information would be quick, but the missing person searches would take time in two other states.

Lott was headed to the DMV before they closed to try to get a trace on the registration of the car.

And she was going to take the receipt addresses and names and see if she could make a pattern of the area where most of the Las Vegas receipts were grouped. Almost all of them were along the Boulder Highway, they knew that much from just looking at them. They had figured that giving them a closer look might give them at least a center to work from.

It was almost six in the evening and the sun was low in the sky by the time she finished out along the highway. Most of the gas stations and grocery stores on the receipts were gone or replaced by newer stations. But the addresses kept everything in a pattern about a mile long.

Clearly he had mostly stayed in this area while here in Las Vegas, but there was little near the area except older subdivisions and a few small casinos and old highway motels that she doubted looked much better in 1992.

And since there were no receipts for a hotel, she didn't bother with them.

But she did cruise a few of the streets of the subdivisions in her Jeep SUV, just looking for anything that might strike her. All the homes were clearly already old in 1992. And there were also a number of older apartment buildings. Most of the neighborhood just looked tired and rundown.

Maybe Stan had family here?

Or a girlfriend?

At the time, Julia had no idea her husband had even came to Las Vegas. And he claimed he hated gambling. But right now she didn't trust anything he had told her.

Or her memory for that matter.

At six, she headed for the Bellagio and the café there to meet Lott for dinner. She really liked talking with him and he seemed to enjoy her company as well.

There was clearly a connection between them and she had no plans on trying to stop that connection. In fact, she wanted to spend even more time with him as this went along.

It took her almost a half hour to get from the Boulder Highway to The Strip and parked and into the Café Bellagio. She was stunned as she walked in that Lott was already there sitting with his daughter, Annie, and Doc Hill, Annie's boyfriend.

Doc and Annie had clearly already eaten, but Lott was just sipping on an iced tea.

As she approached, Annie looked up and smiled. "Detective Rogers," she said.

Doc stood up and shook her hand, smiling. Julia wasn't sure exactly what to say other than "Just Julia."

These two were two of the best poker players in the world

and she had watched them on television and studied their games before even deciding to move to Las Vegas.

They both were tanned from all the time on the river in central Idaho this summer, and Doc was about as handsome as they came. Together, Doc and Annie made a striking couple. Both tall, young, and in great physical shape. They both seemed to just radiate youth and attractiveness, even though neither of them tried for that effect at all.

Julia suddenly felt like a little girl in front of two major movie stars, even though she had talked to them before and Annie had told her about the Cold Poker Gang and introduced Julia to Lott. It was one thing to talk with a person while sitting next to them in a poker game, another to talk with them away from the game.

Annie gave her a quick hug and then she took Doc's hand and said, "Time to go."

"Don't rush off on my account," Julia said.

"Dinner break on the tournament is almost over," Annie said. "I'm short-stacked so I might be back sooner than not."

Now Julia realized what they were doing. It was the regular weekly thousand-dollar buy-in hold'em tournament. She hadn't yet played in it because the entrance fee was still a little high for her budget. And with the focus on the case, she hadn't played any poker besides with the Cold Poker Gang for almost a week.

"We'll be here for a while," Lott said, smiling at his daughter. "Have fun."

"Will do," Annie said.

"Detectives," Doc said, nodding to both of them as he turned and went with his girlfriend back toward the casino and the poker room beyond.

"Those two are really something," Julia said as she settled into a chair facing across the table from Lott.

"And rich," Lott said, laughing. "They fly all over the world in a private jet and you ought to see the home they are building to the north of town. Plus they have a home up in Boise and Doc's father's home here in town."

"Yeah, I heard Doc's father was killed a year or so ago," Julia said.

Lott nodded. "Annie hadn't gone full-time poker yet and was still working part-time as a detective. That case is the reason they met. It was her last official case. Although, the two of them do some freelance work for the police at times."

"Well, I'm glad she introduced me to you," Julia said, smiling at Lott.

He smiled back. "I'm glad she did as well."

They might have sat there just smiling at each other like a couple of kids for the next half hour, but the waiter broke the moment by starting to clean up Doc and Annie's dishes and asked Julia if she wanted something to drink.

She hoped to have more of those moments with Lott in the near future. She was really, really attracted to him.

And for the first time in a very long time, that felt wonderful.

CHAPTER NINE

September, 2014
Bellagio Hotel and Casino
Las Vegas, Nevada

"So, any luck?" Rogers asked him after the waiter had taken her drink order and left with Annie and Doc's dishes. She seemed to be in complete detective mode, leaving the personal out of this case for the moment.

"There were a lot of dark-green 1989 Dodge Caravans in Nevada in 1992," he said, shaking his head. "And none registered to a Rocha."

"So who owned the car?" she asked.

He sighed. "Damn good question. They are sending me a list tomorrow of names of people who owned that kind of van in 1992. I limited the results to the Las Vegas area, which will cut it down a lot to start, but it might not help."

"I have a hunch we can limit it even more," she said, smiling at him.

He loved her smile, but this time it seemed she had some real information she very much wanted to tell him.

"Those receipts were all around a few subdivision and apartment complexes out on the Boulder Highway. Unless Andor comes up with a van that was impounded, my gut sense is the van never moved from that neighborhood after Stan's death."

Lott felt a slight jolt of excitement that he always felt when there was movement on a case. There was a real chance that car might lead them right to some great leads as to what happened to Stan Rocha.

"Let's find out," Lott said, grabbing his cell phone and calling Andor while smiling at Rogers.

"Yeah," Andor said as he picked up his phone. He never answered a phone in any other way.

"Anything on the impound?"

"Nada," Andor said. "You?"

"Nothing registered to Rocha," Lott said, "but tomorrow I got a list of that type of van registered to others in this area coming. And the receipts led Rogers to a clear neighborhood area out on the highway."

"Perfect," Andor said. "Call me in the morning if anything comes together and we'll do a house call."

"Got it," Lott said, hanging up and smiling at Rogers.

"I assume he found nothing on the impound," Rogers said.

"He didn't," Lott said. "But he thinks we might be doing a house call tomorrow."

"Wouldn't that be nice," Rogers said, smiling a smile that Lott knew he would never tire of.

The next two hours were wonderful, with easy talk about both of their careers, her now-deceased parents, and even how she met Rocha.

And she got Lott talking about Carol through desserts of

apple pie for him and a small bowl of vanilla ice cream with chocolate for her. It felt odd to talk about Carol to a woman he was interested in, but at the same time it felt natural. Carol had been his life for a very long time. If he and Julia had any chance of any kind of relationship, he had to be comfortable talking about Carol, and Julia had to be comfortable with that as well.

And she seemed to be completely comfortable.

They were still talking about Carol when Annie joined them, clearly surprised they were talking about her mother.

"You get into the money?" Rogers asked as Annie sat down and indicated to the nearby waiter to bring her a cup of hot black tea.

"Got my entry fee back at tenth is all," Annie said, shaking her head. "Doc is chewing up the tournament as he often does, huge stacks of chips. He took me out like I was so much trash."

"Wow," Lott said, "that sounds harsh."

His daughter laughed in a way that reminded him a lot of her mother. "At a poker table, there is no such thing as being nice to another player."

"I'm learning that on the Tuesday night games," Rogers said, also laughing.

"And taking all of our money at the same time," Lott said.

Annie patted his hand. "Ahh, too bad, dad. She's going to make you guys raise your game."

"She already has," he said, smiling at Rogers, who smiled back.

"So what case are you two working on that's keeping you out so late?"

"We're trying to figure out who killed my ex-husband here in Vegas back in 1992," Rogers said.

Annie just looked at her, blinking.

Lott laughed. It wasn't often Annie could be surprised, but

that statement had done it, especially Rogers' matter-of-fact manner. Annie had lost her well-known poker face, not something she often let slip for any reason.

"It was my first case as a detective," Lott said. "You were about ten."

"The Rocha case?" Annie asked, glancing at Lott first, then back at Rogers.

Annie was showing her few years as a detective and knowledge of her father's cases. But Lott was surprised she remembered the name of the case. Granted, he had talked about it at times. But he hadn't realized Annie knew about it as well.

Rogers nodded. "I kept my maiden name and we were separated when he was killed. Never was much of a marriage."

Annie shook her head. "Didn't realize you were that cop from Reno. I made a slight run at that case in a slow week about a year after I got my shield," she said. "Got almost nowhere. You two having any luck?"

"Almost nowhere?" Lott asked, glancing at Rogers who looked as puzzled as he felt.

Annie nodded. "I went back into the evidence and pulled samples off the stuff they got from under his fingernails. It was mostly rock and dirt particles found to the north and west of the city. It was as if he had been digging out in the desert for some reason. He had the same material on his pants and shirt. All that led nowhere."

Lott nodded and smiled at his daughter. "Good thinking."

"Reports are under a separate file name, I think the file is titled Rocha two. Dated my second year."

"We'll get it," Lott said.

"Frustrating case," Annie said. "You guys make any headway?"

"Looking for his van," Rogers said.

Annie frowned. "I checked the DMV for Nevada and California to see if he had a car. Nothing popped."

"Under another name, clearly," Lott said. "We know the make of the van and we have an area off the Boulder Highway he stayed when in town. And we know he traveled from Reno to Winnemucca to Boise and then to Salt Lake and then here."

"But we have no idea why," Rogers said.

"You guys are making some progress," Annie said, nodding. "A lot more than I managed, that's for sure. Let me know if there's anything Doc and I can do to help."

"Oh, trust me, we will," Lott said, smiling at his daughter.

From there Rogers asked Annie a question about her mother and Lott sat back and listened to his daughter tell a woman he was interested in about his wonderful departed wife.

It didn't get any weirder or more uncomfortable than that.

CHAPTER TEN

September, 2014
Boulder Highway
Las Vegas, Nevada

At ten in the morning, Julia had just finished her morning workout routine, a shower and breakfast, when Lott called.

"Andor and I will meet you in the parking lot of the grocery store on the northeast corner of Tropicana and the Boulder Highway."

"How long?" she asked.

"I'm leaving now," Lott said. "Twenty minutes."

"Got it," she said, and hung up.

She had an apartment down near the university off The Strip, so she was the closest to the corner than any of the three of them.

She strapped on her old badge and put her gun holster on and under her arm. The Cold Poker Gang had permission from the Las Vegas Police Chief, even though retired, to flash badges and carry their guns, since they were investigating murder cases for the department. That privilege came, Lott had told her, from them closing more cold cases than anyone in the history of the department. Which in turn gave the chief a good name and record.

She reached the parking lot first and parked her Jeep SUV off to one side so she could see the others when they came in. This was the neighborhood she had investigated yesterday, so clearly they had a hit on an address for the van.

She could feel the excitement building a little and scolded herself to remain professional. She doubted the van would be around still, but maybe they could get lucky and find someone who remembered who owned it.

She got out into the early morning heat when she saw Lott's Cadillac SUV pull in. It was only eighty degrees, but still felt warm to her for this early in the morning. It was going to be past ninety again today.

She had put on her standard work clothes; dark slacks, white blouse, and business jacket. The jacket hid her gun nicely. She had her hair pulled back and tied out of the way.

Lott pulled up beside her and motioned she should get into the back.

Andor was already in the front seat. Lott must have picked him up on the way.

"This the area you explored last night?" Andor asked as she closed the door.

"Square in the center of all the receipt addresses," she said, settling with relief into the air conditioning coolness.

"Great," Lott said, turning and smiling at her with that smile she was starting to like so much. "The van is registered to a Denise Miller about four blocks from here."

"Is registered?" Julia asked, her stomach twisting.

"Right from 1989 onward," Andor said as Lott took them out of the parking lot and away from the highway 'into the very old and rough subdivision to the east.

She forced herself to sit back and not jump to any conclusions. She focused on studying the houses. They almost all needed paint, none had any more than rocks and weeds for yards, and many of them had cars up on blocks in the driveways. A few of the homes were boarded up with sad-looking For Sale signs hanging in the front yards.

Lott pulled up in front of one house on the left. In the driveway she could see a van identical to her husband's. Only it needed paint badly since the dark green had turned a faded ugly and pitted olive color. It had a badly dented rear panel. And on the driver door there was a horseshoe-shaped dent that she remembered was on Stan's van.

Holy hell, it was his van, and even more amazingly, it looked like it was still being used. How was that even possible?

"I'll be go to hell," Andor said, staring at the van.

"That the van?" Lott asked, turning to look at Julia.

"Looks exactly like it," she said. "Right down to the horseshoe dent on the driver's door."

"How do you want to handle this?" Andor looked at Lott.

"We knock, flash badges, and talk," Lott said.

Andor nodded.

Julia nodded.

"No mention that you're his wife, got it?" Lott said, looking at her with a dark seriousness to his eyes.

"Copy that," she said, nodding.

She was feeling slightly in shock and was glad Lott was leading this. She couldn't believe they had found Stan's van. It hadn't even occurred to her to look for it after he died, and now because of a few receipts and some legwork with the DMV, they had found it twenty-two years later.

It didn't get any more amazing than that.

They climbed out and made it up the gravel sidewalk to the front door through the warming morning air without saying a word between them.

She forced herself to take slow, deep breaths of the warm air and stay in detective mode.

Andor banged on the screen door that hadn't seen a screen in a decade, let alone paint. The rest of the house looked just as bad, and the windows hadn't been cleaned in a decade. Moisture-stained drapes hid any look at the inside the house.

Julia stayed behind Lott, since there wasn't room for all three of them on the small concrete slab that served for a step up into the house.

She and Lott both scanned the front of the house in both directions. Old training kicking in, clearly.

After a moment a young man answered, maybe college age at most, swinging the door wide open.

"Yes?" he asked, his voice deep and exactly like Stan's voice.

Julia gasped and stepped back. The kid in front of them could have been Stan when she met him. Same dark hair, same dark eyes, same voice. This kid had on a UNLV tee shirt and jeans.

He was going to the same school as Jane, his half-sister.

Lott glanced back at her, clearly worried at the sound and more than likely the shocked look on her face.

"Your mother or father home?" Andor asked, flashing his badge.

Julia noticed that as Andor introduced all three of them as detectives, he made sure that he flashed his gun under his jacket in the process.

The kid stammered for a moment, then turned and shouted, "Mom?"

A woman about Julia's age appeared. She had bleached-blonde hair pulled back and was wearing a MGM Grand Hotel room service uniform. She was very thin and clearly smoked, since through the open door and hole where the screen used to be, a smoke-smell wafted over them.

Andor again introduced all three of them as she stood there, nodding.

"Are you Denise Miller?" Lott asked.

"I am," she said, nodding.

"You own that van?" Lott asked, pointing at the van.

"I do," she said. "But it mostly goes only between here and MGM. It's seen its day. Why?"

"We're actually looking for information about a man who used to drive it by the name of Stan Rocha."

At that, Denise Miller did something Julia would have never thought would be a response.

Denise laughed. A smoker's laugh, rough and ending in a cough.

Then Denise Miller said something that sent Julia back one more step.

"Someone finally dig up the body of that worthless husband of mine? After twenty-two years, it's about damn time."

Then the kid beside Denise asked Lott, "You found my father? Really?"

All Julia could do was gasp for the thin hot air and try to focus, as she had learned how to do over decades as a detective.

In fact, without that training, more than likely she'd just be sitting on the sidewalk right now.

She felt like doing that anyhow, but managed to remain

standing and staring at a woman that had been married to her husband at the same time she was.

And had a son with him as well.

Luckily, that son-of-a-bitch husband of theirs was dead. He wasn't the type to face this kind of thing easily, even though this was all his mess.

And mess didn't begin to describe this.

CHAPTER ELEVEN

September, 2014
Just off the Boulder Highway
Las Vegas, Nevada

Andor, putting on his charm offensive as Lott had seen him do many times over the years, asked Denise Miller if they could talk with her.

She said sure. She said she had an hour before she had to be to work. She indicated they come in and took her son's arm and pushed him back inside away from the front door.

Lott stepped back and took Rogers' elbow. Then he whispered to her. "You okay? You want to wait in the car?"

She shook her head and took a deep breath, clearly finding a way to center and ground herself as all good detectives could do. "I'll be fine," she whispered back.

Lott wasn't so sure how fine she would be. She had just learned that her former husband had been a bigamist and had a son. That kind of news would send anyone spinning. And from what he could tell from Rogers' eyes, she was clearly in slight shock.

"You sure?" he asked.

"Fine," she said, her voice firm. With that she came back into her eyes and looked into his.

He nodded. With that she squared her shoulders, took a deep breath, and stepped up and followed Andor into the smoke-smelling small living room.

She stood to one side, leaning against the wall near the door as Lott followed Andor around and sat on the cloth couch that had seen far more wear than Lott wanted to think about as he sank down into the soft brown cushions.

Denise sat in a big, worn recliner facing a large-screen television and the kid went over and stood behind her and to one side. She didn't pop up the footrest, but instead sat almost sideways in the big chair, facing the couch.

The room was cluttered with old music albums and a few other chairs covered in papers and a couple of shirts.

The place was clearly lived in and seldom cleaned. The drapes over the two windows kept out any hint of sunshine and the smell of bacon mixed with the smoke smell.

"We need some basics, first, if you don't mind," Andor said, putting his nicest smile that had a way of making people relax a little, especially women about his age. He took out a notebook and opened it to a blank page.

Lott didn't move and neither did Rogers. It was normal for only one detective to take notes in situations like this. This time it would be Andor. Lott was glad he was, since Lott was worried about Rogers.

Denise smiled at Andor and said, "Sure, fire away."

Lott managed to not laugh. Andor could charm a woman without hardly trying, so when he turned it on, the women he interviewed seemed to just melt for him. And it certainly wasn't because of his looks.

"You were married to Stan Rocha from when to when?" Andor asked.

"From the spring of 1988 to the day he disappeared in 1992," she said. "I guess technically I'm still married to the jerk unless you find his body or something."

"I'm sorry to have to tell you, but Stan Rocha was killed in May of 1992," Andor said fairly bluntly. "He was shot and left in a warehouse downtown."

"Shit," the kid said, his voice rough.

Denise just shook her head. "I always sort of knew he was dead, but didn't hear about that. I don't read the papers much. I figured one of his lost mines had killed him with a cave-in or something."

"Lost mines?" Andor asked.

Lott was very glad Andor asked that question or he would have. Out of the corner of his eye he saw Rogers stand up away from the wall.

"Sure, that's all he did. He searched for lost treasure and lost mines. He called it his job and figured that any day he would strike it rich. He was sometimes gone for a month out there in those deserts. So he was shot, huh? And I assume, since you are here now, you never found out who did it."

Lott started to open his mouth, then closed it. He glanced over at Rogers who looked just as shocked as he felt. Why would an old buried treasure or lost gold mine get Rocha executed?

"Anyone who would want him dead back then?" Andor asked.

Denise shook her head. "He was a freeloader, of that there was no doubt. He hated anything that looked or smelled like real work. But he was a general nice guy, docile as a lamb, too much at times."

Lott again noticed that Rogers was nodding slightly. That was similar to some things Rogers had said about Stan as well.

"Unless he ran across something in the desert that he shouldn't have," Denise said, "I can't imagine why anyone would kill him. He didn't gamble and had no money except what little I gave him to keep him going searching for mines."

"You have any of his research material," Andor asked. "That might help us a lot discover what got him killed."

"Oh, sure," Denise said. "Boxes of the stuff that was in his closet, his desk, and mostly the van. We sold all his picks and shovels and stuff, but kept all the paperwork."

"So you ever try to figure out where he vanished?" Andor asked.

Denise laughed. "He'd been gone almost two months when I really started to think something was wrong. When I looked at his paperwork, he was digging into lost treasures all over Nevada and into Idaho and Utah. No clue where he was. And he never told me much of anything, to be honest. Tightlipped guy. When he didn't come back, I just figured he either had bailed on me and his new baby, or a cave-in got him."

"Sorry to bring you the bad news," Andor said, keeping his charm on full burn. Lott figured it was going to be lucky they got out of there without this woman offering to take Andor into the back room by the time he was finished. Over the years, Andor had had a lot of those offers, but never once took a woman up on it. He had been devoted to Helen, his now-dead wife, and never once gave any of the offers even a second thought.

Denise just shrugged. "As far as we were concerned, he's been dead a long time."

The kid nodded, but Lott could tell he was shocked. Before this visit he had a father lost in a mine cave-in, not shot in a murder.

"If you wouldn't mind getting all of Rocha's stuff for us," Andor said, smiling and standing. "We'll let you get on to work."

She smiled and stood, giving the look to Andor that Lott knew was an "I'm single, call me" look.

"Do you know where my dad is buried?" the kid asked.

Lott nodded. "I'll have the directions brought over."

Denise patted her son's arm, clearly understanding that he was having some trouble with all this.

"Come on, Roger," she said to her son. "Let's get your father's stuff for these detectives."

Lott started to open her mouth, then said nothing. He turned to Rogers, who was staring at the kid.

Then she said softly to Lott, "I'll wait in the car."

After she was out the door, Lott turned to Denise. "I don't mean to pry, but why did you name your son Roger?"

"Stan said it was on old family name and I liked it," she said. "Roger wasn't even a year old when his father disappeared."

"Sorry, for the bad news, kid," Andor said.

"Just find who killed him," Roger said.

"That's what we hope to do," Lott said. "And we'll keep you informed when we do."

"Thanks," Denise said, leading them to a closet at the end of a narrow hallway where she had stored the six boxes of Stan Rocha's work.

Boxes that might just get them closer to who killed him. If they were lucky.

And Lott knew at this point they were going to have to be very lucky.

CHAPTER TWELVE

September, 2014
Off the Boulder Highway
Las Vegas, Nevada

As they carried out the boxes from Denise Miller's house to his car through the warming morning air, Lott decided he had a couple more quick questions to ask Denise.

"Did Rocha have another car besides using your van?"

"Sure," she said, nodding as they reached the back of the Cadillac and he got the back gate open. "It was a 1985 Chevy Impala. Nasty green color. But he liked taking the van when heading out in to the desert for any kind of long trip. He said it allowed him to sleep in the van if he needed to."

Andor nodded to Lott at the answer to that question as he put a box in the back of the Cadillac and turned to Denise. "So he took the Impala the day he left here and never came back?"

"He did," she said, nodding as she took a box from her son and handed it to Andor to put in the back of the Cadillac.

Rogers was turned around slightly in the back seat listening. Lott hoped she was doing all right. He would know soon enough, but he couldn't imagine how she could be. Her dead husband had another family and had named his son after her. Didn't get much weirder than that.

"So do you know if he had any family other than the Rogers?" Lott asked.

"Oh, sure," Denise said, smiling at Andor. "His parents and brother live in Boise. I called them a few years ago to see if they had heard from Stan and they hadn't. They were both still alive, as well as Stan's brother, still in Boise. Now I know why they hadn't heard from him. But honestly, he and his parents were never close, at least that's what he told me."

"You got their number and names?" Andor asked, giving Denise his biggest smile.

"Sure, come on back into the house and I'll get it for you with the last couple of boxes."

Andor nodded and followed Denise and her son back into the house.

Lott watched him go and hoped that Denise would let Andor out of there with his pants on.

Rogers was shaking her head. She got out and moved around behind the Cadillac with Lott. He wanted to touch her elbow, but it was clear she had her footing again and was doing all right.

Or at least as well as possible considering all the weird things she had just learned.

"This is making no sense at all," she said, glancing back to make sure Denise and Andor had not yet come back out of the house. "How come on the police report I was listed as his wife? And she was never notified?"

"I honestly don't remember," Lott said. "But I agree, we

need to find that out. It doesn't make sense. Not a lick of sense, actually, since she was here in town."

At that moment, Andor and Denise came back out, both carrying another old brown file box.

Lott took the one from Denise and put it in the back of the Cadillac while Andor did the same with the other box. They all just about filled the back area of the SUV.

"One more question if you don't mind," Lott said, remembering one more detail they needed to know. "Did Rocha have any family in Salt Lake or Winnemucca?"

Denise looked puzzled, then shook her head. "None that I knew of. He said his best friend, a woman by the name of Julia, lived in Reno. But he didn't say much else beyond that about any other family or friends outside of Boise."

"Thanks," Andor said, reaching out and shaking her hand and smiling, holding onto her hand just a little longer than he needed to, another of his many tricks. "I hope you don't mind if I call you if we need more questions answered."

"Any time, detective," she said, smiling back at Andor as Lott took Julia's elbow and got her around to the back seat and then closed the door. She looked to be in complete shock, and Lott didn't blame her at all.

Andor waved at Denise from the passenger seat as Lott got them headed down the road.

Then Andor turned back to stare at Rogers. "You all right?"

"I've been better," she said, her voice firm and clearly angry. "But I'll be fine. The bastard's been dead for over twenty years after all. Lucky for him."

"Yeah," Andor said, turning around and giving Lott a high-eyebrow look. "Doesn't make it sting any less."

"Got that right," Rogers said.

CHAPTER THIRTEEN

September, 2014
Off of the Boulder Highway
Las Vegas, Nevada

Julia felt like she was in shock as Lott took them back through the subdivision toward her car. She wasn't completely sure she could drive at the moment, and she needed to get her feet under her from all this new information about her former husband.

She always knew she had never really known him, but now she was questioning everything about her own judgment.

How could she have missed so much?

What in the world had been wrong with her?

She needed answers now a lot more than she had when she suggested they start down this road.

Lott glanced back at her, then said, "Anyone up for some lunch?"

"Wendy's," Andor said. "One about a half mile in toward town."

Rogers smiled. He was taking care of her. And right now she really appreciated that.

Lott laughed and then looked back at her. "You like Wendy's hamburgers, Rogers?"

"Not so much," she said, "but I love their chicken sandwich and their baked potatoes. So it sounds perfect. Thanks."

"Wendy's it is," Lott said, nodding. He went past the parking lot with her car and turned onto the Boulder Highway.

In ten minutes they were ordering and were shortly tucked off at a table to one side. The lunch rush was still a good forty-five minutes away, so no one was sitting close to them at all.

She was very glad for this idea of lunch. She was already feeling better. Lott really seemed to already know her. And part of her really liked that, and that he cared enough to figure out something to help like this.

They all made small talk for a few minutes while they dug into their sandwiches and hamburgers and fries. Cops were notorious for not eating well and clearly the three of them weren't that concerned even after decades of being in the field. But she had to admit, Wendy's food was one of the best in the fast food world. But it was still fast food.

Finally Lott reached down and pulled up the yellow legal pad he had brought in with him. "We need to get a plan going on this."

"We're making a ton more progress than I thought we would," Andor said, also getting out his notebook. Then he looked at her. "Sorry, Rogers, for the hit this is causing you."

"Lott asked me if I wanted to open up this part of my past," she said. "I know digging into cold cases is often like turning over a pile of rotted and molding boards and seeing what bugs scatter. So I can handle it. Just ignore me if I stagger for a moment."

Andor laughed.

"Deal," Lott said.

"So what's next?" she said before taking another bite of her chicken sandwich. She was surprised that it actually had some chicken flavor to it and a nice light pepper kick. She remembered it being good, just not this good. Not something you normally get in fast food.

"I still have missing persons searching old files in Winnemucca, Boise, and Salt Lake," Andor said. "Those might be in sometime this afternoon."

"I think we should run a pretty good check on that Denise Miller," Lott said. "She might know a lot more than she's letting on. I wouldn't put it past her to have put three shots in Rocha when she discovered he was married to Julia."

"I agree," Andor said.

Julia was glad that neither one of them had asked her opinion on that. She thought they needed to do the same thing, but coming from her it might have sounded off. And she wasn't sure if it was her gut instinct or old feelings that had her thinking that something about Denise Miller felt off.

"What about the building he was found in?" she asked. "Now that we know Rocha was into mining and old treasures, would the owners of that building back in 1992 have a connection anywhere else in the state? It was a mining company that owned it, right?"

Lott nodded and looked at Andor, who was also nodding. Then they both added that to their notes.

"We always wondered why he ended up there," Lott said, "and how anyone knew it was empty and unlocked. I know exactly who to help us with that search."

"Who?" she asked.

"Annie and Doc," Lott said.

Andor nodded.

"Why them?" she asked.

"They have some amazing ways of getting information and links buried in old files," Lott said. "Far more than we have. Not sure if it's completely legal and I honestly don't want to know."

Julia was surprised. She knew that Annie and Doc sometimes helped on cases, but she didn't know that. "How did they get that ability?"

"Money," Andor said, shaking his head. "More money than anyone else in this city, actually. More money than two good-looking people of that age should ever have."

"I wouldn't know about that," Lott said, laughing. "But they made some contacts when they were working on his father's death."

"Same one where the President's friend and Chief of Staff were killed?" Julia asked.

"Same one," Lott said.

She dropped the subject at that. If Lott trusted his daughter and Doc to get the information, then they were good as far as she was concerned.

"So we also need to put traces and impound searches on that Impala," Andor said.

"Back to the DMV for me," Lott said. "They love me there."

"I'll check the missing persons," Andor said, "and get someone going on the impound of the Impala, see if that happened."

"What do you need me to do?" Julia asked.

Lott glanced at Andor. "Head home, take a nap for about two hours, change into your sorting clothes, and meet me and Andor back at my place in three hours. We have a lot of boxes to sort."

She appreciated the thought. And she planned on doing part

of it. "Tell you what. I'll only take an hour-long nap to get my feet under me, then get on the internet and see what I can find for books on lost mines and treasures around this part of Nevada."

"Perfect," Andor said. "And check the old bookstore down on the corner of Sahara and Industrial. Who knows what they might have as well. Those folks in there seem to know more about Nevada history than anyone in the state."

"That I can do," she said. "Someone is going to have to contact his parents and let them know their son is dead."

Lott glanced at Andor.

"Let's wait until we have a few more answers first," Andor said.

She agreed and nodded her thanks to Lott, then quickly finished off her chicken sandwich in two bites as the other two stood.

Typical. She was always the last one still eating. Especially with other detectives.

Over the years, she had left many a meal half-eaten. At least these two were kind enough to let her get close to the end before heading to the door.

CHAPTER FOURTEEN

September, 2014
Pleasant Hills
Las Vegas, Nevada

Julia arrived at Lott's home and parked out front of the well-kept two-story home. It was clearly a loved place with a green lawn and desert plants arranged with care in great patterns in rock gardens. Lott hadn't gotten there yet, since his car wasn't in the carport attached to the house where he normally parked it.

More than likely he had gotten hung up at the DMV. She didn't envy him that task. She had spent her time in the DMV up in Reno over the years. They had been friendly people, at least in Reno, and she always bought them small Christmas presents every year.

But even with nice people, the task of searching old databases was never easy or fun.

Before she came over, she had managed to find a good dozen books on lost treasures and mines in Nevada online, and a few more that covered the entire Southwest, from California over through Utah and Arizona. Stan had no receipts from Arizona, so she had ignored books on that state. She had managed to get three of the main ones she had found online from the bookstore that Lott had suggested. One, a book titled *Nevada: Lost Mines and Buried Treasures* by McDonald had been published in 1981 before she had met Stan, so it might have been one of the books he used. Or at least knew about.

It would give them a start if they found an area he might be working.

Earlier, after getting back to her apartment, she had actually made herself lie down for a short time. That, and the lunch, had helped her get her mind back and she now felt fine again.

She supposed it shouldn't have surprised her that Stan had another wife. As Denise had said, he was a freeloader.

For all she knew, Stan also had wives in Winnemucca and Salt Lake. Now if she and Lott found them, those extra wives wouldn't surprise her. If he had to marry while freeloading, that would only make sense. He clearly had had the ability to remember who he was with at any time and keep his stories and different lives straight.

But what bothered her a lot was why they had called her as his wife and not Denise, right here in town. That made no sense at all.

And why he had named his son after her? He hadn't lived long enough to have anything to do with naming Jane. He was dead before she had been born, so Julia had named her new baby daughter after her own mother.

Now she was going to have to tell her daughter that her father had been a bigamist and that she had a half-brother about her age.

That wasn't a conversation she was looking forward to.

Over twenty years after his death, Stan was still driving her crazy.

At that moment, Lott pulled into his driveway, waving at her and smiling through the tinted windows as he went past.

Just seeing him made her smile. She couldn't believe that at her age she was falling again for someone. She couldn't even remember how this had felt all those years ago, before meeting Stan.

She hadn't even felt this way with Stan. He had just been someone easy to hang around with, who didn't mind her being a cop, and who was pretty decent in bed. She had a hunch that if she really looked at it, she used him as much as he used her.

It would have been nice, though, if he could have helped raise Jane some. But he clearly hadn't lived long enough to even know that Jane was coming along. Julia had planned on telling him the next time he was in town. But instead got a phone call about his murder.

She climbed out into the late afternoon heat. It was just around 3:30 and the temperature in late September still had to be over ninety, easily. She had no doubt this heat and weather were going to take her a few years to get used to.

She moved up behind Lott's white Cadillac as he climbed out and opened the back hatch. Then he went to open the back-door as she reached for the first brown box.

It was light, so she grabbed another and took two into the back door and the coolness of the kitchen.

"Where shall I stack them?" she asked.

"Against the wall in the kitchen dining area," he said, going past her for a load.

Clearly this wasn't anywhere near the first time he had done something like this.

Working quickly, they had the nine brown file boxes out of

the car and into the coolness of the dining area. The boxes were clearly dirty and smelled of smoke after all the years in Denise's home.

"You have some fresh boxes?" she asked. She had spent her years in and out of smoke in bars and restaurants and people's homes, but there was still nothing worse than the smell of smoke built up on paper and cardboard over decades of time. It had a rich, thick, rank smell like something long spoiled.

He wrinkled his nose and nodded, turning toward an area off the kitchen that looked like a storage room.

He came back a moment later with a stack of ten fresh file boxes from Staples, not yet put together.

They quickly put the boxes together, dumping the contents of each of Stan's boxes into a fresh one without looking at any of it and then tossing the old box outside into the carport.

It only took a few minutes and when they were done and had lids on the boxes, the smoke smell was mostly gone.

"Much better," he said, nodding, clearly relieved. "Good idea."

Then he stopped, faced her, and looked her squarely in the eyes.

She was again startled at how intense his gaze was and how handsome he was when he looked at her like that.

"Are you all right?"

"Honestly," she said, "that was a shock, especially the part where he named his kid after me. But I'm fine now. Got past it."

"You sure?" he asked, clearly worried, as she would have been in his spot.

"Completely sure," she said. "It's been over two decades after all that he's been dead. I didn't like him much anymore when he was killed."

"Fair enough," he said, still looking into her eyes with that fantastic gaze of his.

"But there is one thing I need," she said, looking at him with her most intent stare, as if she was going to ask him for the secrets of the world.

"Anything," he said, being very serious right back.

"A glass of that wonderful iced tea of yours."

Then she smiled.

It took him an instant, but then he laughed, shaking his head as he turned toward the fridge. "Yup, you're fine."

With that she laughed, and honestly, that felt great after how the day had already gone.

CHAPTER FIFTEEN

September, 2014
Pleasant Hills
Las Vegas, Nevada

Lott enjoyed the feeling as he and Rogers settled in with their iced teas and starting looking through the boxes from Denise Miller's home. He was very glad Rogers was going to be all right. He had worried about her all afternoon since leaving her at her car.

And when he realized he was worrying about her, he felt startled and surprised. It was the same kind of worry he used to feel about Carol. A kind of worry that was anchored in actually caring for a person.

They started off by sorting receipts again, making sure that all the receipts were in the four major areas that they knew about, plus another pile for the ones they couldn't read or that were not in Winnemucca, Boise, or Salt Lake.

They tossed the Reno and Las Vegas receipts back into a

fresh box unless it was something unusual or that they couldn't figure out.

They put all the maps and books and notebooks into another box. They were through the second box and had the third one dumped out on the table when Andor banged on the front door.

"Open!" Lott shouted and Andor came in, stomping through the living room like he always did.

Lott glanced at Rogers who was smiling much like Carol used to smile every time Andor did that. Andor sounded more like a monster approaching than a retired detective.

"Any luck at the DMV?" Andor asked as he came in and went to the fridge to get a bottle of water.

"Nothing," Lott said. "But they are running the same searches they did on the van on the Impala for me. They'll have it tomorrow."

"So he didn't own that car either," Andor said, shaking his head and sitting down at the end of the kitchen table.

"How about you?" Rogers asked.

"No Impala impounded anywhere around the city from 1992 to 1995. Nothing. So I have running searches for the car in other areas outside of the metro limits."

"Good," Lott said. "And I called Annie and asked her to search the records of the building and compare it to outside interests of any type. She said that she and Doc and their friend Fleet would get right on it."

"So we have a ton of irons in this fire," Andor said.

Lott couldn't agree more. A lot more than he had expected them to have at this point. He half expected them to be playing cards every week with no leads at all.

Now, as Andor sat down and took a long drink from the bottle of water, Lott could tell his partner wasn't giving all the information. After working together for almost twenty years, he knew that look on Andor's face.

"So spit out the rest," Lott said, pretending to sort receipts and not look at Andor.

"Sometimes you are a damn kill-joy," Andor said.

Lott glanced up at Rogers' smiling face and winked.

"We got two hits on the missing persons search," Andor said, smiling. "One four months after Rocha's death in Winnemucca and another the same month in Salt Lake."

Then he frowned and looked at Rogers.

"Let me guess, both were from his wives," she said, shaking her head in disgust.

"Got that in one," Andor said. "Sorry."

Lott stared at Rogers, who clearly didn't seem to be bothered by it. And from what he had seen of her over the last four months, she didn't have that good of an emotional poker face.

"It's starting to figure," Rogers said. "And after this morning I expected it."

"How's that?" Lott asked, clearly puzzled as to why Rogers was now taking this news so well.

"He was a freeloader, plain and simple," Rogers said. "And he was in search of some lost treasure. No sane woman was going to let him do that and help support him unless he married her. And more than likely if he had even told me what he was doing, I'd have booted his ass down the road sooner than I was doing."

Lott had to admit that she was right on that.

Andor looked at her, frowning. "Are you saying it's one thing for a husband to be a freeloader, another for a boyfriend to be one?"

"You got it," she said. "Women won't stay with freeloaders

very long as boyfriends. Husbands who don't work are as common as sand on the beach."

Lott had to agree with her on that as well. He'd seen that more times then he wanted to think about.

"Got any idea how long he was doing this sort of thing?" Andor asked.

"I got a hunch these boxes are going to help answer some of that question," Rogers said, pointing to the stack of banker boxes. "But I don't think he was any older than me when we met, so it had to only have been a little over four years at most. Maybe a few more, but it would take a few years to come up with this kind of plan I would think."

"Denise said she met and married him in 1988," Andor said.

"Same year for me."

"So what do we do about these other wives?" Andor asked.

"Same thing we do with his parents in Boise," Lott said. "We wait and see what else we can come up with first."

Suddenly Lott noticed that Rogers frowned and sat back.

"Something wrong?"

She laughed. "With this case, just damn near everything. You have the official police file on this?"

"On the counter over there," Lott said, pointing toward the stove. "And I got the second one that Annie started as well with it."

Andor and Lott went back to sorting the paper on the table as Rogers moved over to the file. After a moment she said, "I thought I remembered that."

"What?" Lott asked.

"Small caliber killed him."

"Twenty-two," Andor said, nodding. "More than likely from a rifle at fairly close range."

"Twenty-two rifles are often used as saddle rifles," she said.

"You thinking he might have been on horseback when he was shot?"

She shook her head. "No idea. But just thinking that a twenty-two is an odd weapon choice to kill someone in an execution-style murder in a city like Las Vegas."

Lott nodded. She was right about that. It was very odd for downtown Las Vegas. But now that they knew Rocha spent time out in the desert, it was less and less odd.

Rogers sat at the table and looked at both of them. "So, tell me, gentlemen, why did you call me as his wife and none of the rest of the other women he was mooching off?"

"I thought about that and looked it up," Andor said, scooting back his chair and going for the official file by the stove. He flipped it open, went in a couple of pages and then pulled out a sheet.

He handed it to Rogers who stared at it for a moment.

"Rocha's driver's license on him when he was killed was issued in Reno," Andor said. "He had you down as wife and next of kin."

"I'll be," she said, shaking her head and handing Andor back the paper.

Then she turned to Lott. "Did the DMV have a statewide database on driver's licenses in 1992?"

"Sure," Lott said. "But I'm betting that Rocha had no issue at that point getting fake driver's licenses for each family. My gut sense is that the license for Reno was the only real one. Or the one he had on him because his next stop was Reno."

"So where did those extra licenses end up?" Andor asked.

That question stunned Lott and he grabbed his notebook and quickly wrote it down.

"He must have had a place all his own somewhere," Rogers

said, shaking her head. "But I have no idea how he could have afforded that."

"Nope," Lott said, suddenly having a flash of insight. He smiled at his two friends. "I know exactly where all his secret stuff is stashed."

"Where?" Andor asked.

Rogers looked at him just as puzzled.

"Tell me if I'm wrong," Lott said. "We're dealing with a guy here who liked to be taken care of, right?"

Rogers nodded. "He liked it when I made the decisions for him like what to eat or what to wear somewhere."

"And from what I saw of Denise this morning," Lott said, "she would have treated him the same way."

"Mother," Rogers said, nodding.

Lott smiled. "We'll find all his secret stuff stashed safely at his home where his mother could take care of it all."

"Looks like someone's going to Boise sooner rather than later," Andor said.

"As soon as we get this all done and find out some results of some ongoing searches," Lott said.

He had a hunch they were just starting to scratch the surface of this case. And going to Boise would only be part of the key to who killed this freeloading bigamist.

And with four known wives, there was now some pretty clear motive. Men over the centuries had been killed for a lot less.

PART TWO

CHAPTER SIXTEEN

October, 2014
Foothills
Boise, Idaho

Doc Hill's big Cadillac SUV rode in silent comfort as Lott drove it slowly up the winding road into the foothills above Boise. Doc had let them use it because, as he said, it was just sitting in his garage doing nothing.

Lott couldn't believe how beautiful this town was, and how rich. The higher they went up the hill, the bigger the homes seemed to get. The home they were looking for was a mansion, plain and simple. He had been to Boise once before and liked it, but clearly he hadn't seen much of it.

Beside him, Rogers rode silently, staring at the homes and huge lawns and carefully trimmed shrubs and shaking her head. She was clearly as surprised as he was about how much money they were driving past.

"You know your in-laws were this rich?" Lott asked as they finally stopped in front of one of the highest and largest homes on the entire street. It had a tall black iron fence around it and monitored gate across the driveway. From what Lott could tell, the driveway wound through some trees farther up the ridgeline to a circular driveway in front of a three-story mansion that could hold a dozen of his homes and not even break a seam.

"Not a clue," Rogers said. "I didn't know I had in-laws, actually. Stan seemed poor and acted poor right down to every detail. For heaven's sake, he drove a three-year-old van with a dent in the door."

Lott just shook his head as they sat there in the comfort of the big car, letting the air-conditioning keep them cool in the afternoon heat of early October. None of this made any sense.

From the moment they started finding out about Stan's many wives, nothing seemed to add up. And they weren't one inch closer to who might have killed him. And they had a lot more questions than answers, now. And a lot of suspects, none of whom felt right to Lott.

They never did find the Impala. It wasn't impounded and there were a lot of them registered in those years after his death, but not to anyone that seemed connected to the case in any way.

And the boxes had been full of receipts and maps and charts and old books. Until they got an exact lead, the maps and such would make no sense. As Andor had said, the boxes were more of a lost treasure than anything Rocha had been looking for.

And then, when Annie and Doc came back with the results of their search on the building, it turned out they had discovered that Stan had actually owned the warehouse where his body had been found.

That had shocked Rogers almost as much as finding out Stan had other wives. Maybe even a bit more.

Stan's company had specialized in mineral rights, which explained a lot of the old maps and documents they found at Denise's home. The company owned upwards of fifty parcels of land around Nevada and had bought mineral rights on a hundred more.

And almost all the holdings were of land where a supposed lost mine or treasure might be located. Stan really had been searching for lost treasure, but doing it with a big corporation.

There didn't seem to be any other shareholders in the company, at least that Annie and Doc could find. All records were privately held in the Nevada corporation. And Nevada, being a state that prided itself on being business friendly and nonintrusive into corporate affairs, didn't have any records other than that Stan was the majority shareholder and ran the company and was the only name on all the documents.

After Stan's death, the company went on for another dozen years and then was finally bought by a mining consortium for an undisclosed amount of money in 2005. They could find no idea as to who got the money or Stan's shares.

Annie and Doc and their crew of researchers had no idea what the company did except buy land, mineral rights, a few water rights, and a dozen different warehouses. But Annie had promised him that they would keep digging.

Annie had gotten interested in the case, since she also had made a run at it when she was a detective. So when Lott told her that they needed to get up to Boise to visit Stan's parents and brother, she and Doc offered to fly them up on their private jet. The two of them had a tournament they had planned to play in at the Bellagio, so they couldn't go along. Which left the private jet with its huge brown leather seats, soft carpet, and wonderful food served by a woman named April to just Lott and Rogers.

Lott had to admit, that was the type of flying he could get

used to. Annie and Doc had offered a few times over the last year to take Lott on a flight, but until this case, he had had no real need to leave Las Vegas.

Now he might find more reasons.

Rogers flat loved the plane, at one point over a glass of wine saying she needed to play more poker.

Lott knew that this jet had been earned by Doc being such a good poker player, but more of it was because his best friend, Fleet, knew how to invest and make money grow. Lott knew the two had been a team since they were in college together, Doc making the cash from poker, and Fleet investing it.

Then when Doc's father had been killed, Doc had inherited another not-so-small fortune.

Lott had asked Annie once how much money Doc had. She had laughed and said, "Trust me, Dad. You don't want to even know."

And now, with the help of Fleet as well, Annie's winnings at poker were making her wealthy as well. Carol would be proud of her daughter, Lott was sure. He sure was.

He glanced over at Rogers who was just staring at the gate of the big mansion. "You ready, Detective?"

She took a deep breath and nodded. "Take the lead," she said.

"Glad to," he said, climbing out into the dry, warm air. It wasn't as warm as Vegas, but still plenty warm enough.

They moved up to the big gate. There was no sign, only an address.

Lott pointed at the bell beside the gate with a speaker above it. "Andor would hate this."

Rogers laughed. "No place to knock."

Lott smiled at her. She would be fine. The two of them had

really come to like spending time together over the last week, mostly eating dinners together. And the flight up here this morning, besides being in luxury, was comfortable between them as well.

He just hoped that once this case was over, they could continue spending time together. He was starting to enjoy not eating alone every evening while getting to know her.

"Yes," a voice came back through the speaker.

"Detectives Lott and Rogers," Lott said into the speaker.

"I'll be right down," the man's voice said.

Lott glanced at Rogers. That was not at all what he had expected. They had called ahead and made an appointment to talk with Carl Rocha, Stan's brother.

And they had both hoped to have a word with Stan's parents as well.

A man looking to be in his late fifties came striding down the driveway. He was dressed in tan golf slacks, a tan short-sleeved golf shirt, and brown loafers.

"Stan's brother," Rogers whispered. "The likeness is scary."

Lott nodded as the gate opened.

Carl Rocha introduced himself with a firm handshake, then asked, "Would you mind if we talk in your car?"

Lott shrugged and turned and led the way. He had Carl climb into the front seat and Rogers climbed into the back behind Lott. She moved to the middle so she could see Carl as well between the big front bucket seats.

Lott turned in his seat so he could see both Carl and Rogers.

"Sorry," Carl said after Lott got the car started and air-conditioning going. "Mom's having a rough day and I didn't want to upset her anymore."

"We understand," Lott said. "Thanks for seeing us."

Carl then did something that Lott was not expecting. He looked back at Rogers. "I assume you are one of Stan's wives? The Detective from Reno?"

All Rogers could do was nod.

How the hell had he known that?

CHAPTER SEVENTEEN

October, 2014
Foothills
Boise, Idaho

Julia sat there stunned for a moment at Carl's question.

"You are correct," she said. "I was Stan's wife in Reno. I was the one informed about his death. I didn't know he had family, let alone other wives. He never mentioned a thing about his life, otherwise I would have contacted you at once."

Carl nodded. "I know you would have, Detective." He then asked the next logical question that Julia would expect a rich person with a mess on his hands to ask.

"Why investigate my brother's death now?"

Lott explained about the group of mostly retired detectives who worked on cold cases for the Las Vegas Police. "Your brother's case was my first case to go cold as a detective. So I have a personal interest in getting it solved."

"And I joined into the group when I retired and moved to

Las Vegas," Julia said. "So how did you know about your brother having a number of wives?"

Carl shrugged. "He told me."

"You're kidding?" Julia asked, again shocked. "That's not like people who do that sort of thing. They are usually very secretive about it. Did he tell you why?"

Carl nodded. "Sure. He said he loved you all and just couldn't help it. Honestly, I tried to get him to get professional help, but he didn't want it. I just kept hoping that the house of cards he was building with all four of you wouldn't come crashing down."

Julia laughed slightly and Lott glanced at her with his worried look she was starting to really like.

"That makes sense for the Stan I knew," she said. "He hated hurting anyone's feelings. He would rather just go along with something instead of complain at all."

Carl nodded. "That was my brother. From a distance I sort of kept track of all four of you for a time after he disappeared. Stopped about ten years ago after it was clear Stan wasn't coming back either here or to any of you."

"And I assume you have kept this all from your parents?" Lott asked.

"I kept everything about his four wives from them except this news about his death," Carl said. "I didn't know he had been murdered until I got a call from Denise Miller after you spoke to her. I told my parents then that Stan was dead. I think they knew, but having it confirmed really set them back. Especially mom. She somehow, after twenty years, kept thinking he would walk in the door at any moment."

Julia couldn't think of anything to say to that.

"We met Denise," Lott said after a moment of silence.

Carl nodded. "She's a real piece of work, that one. Never

met her, but the phone calls are always interesting. She's the only wife Stan told about his parents."

"Do your parents know they have grandkids?" Julia asked.

"I have three kids," Carl said. "At the moment that's enough for them. Detective, realize my father has Alzheimer's and doesn't remember anyone anymore and my mother has congestive heart failure. Both of them have very little time to live. I see no point at this time in their lives to change anything."

Julia nodded. "That honestly makes sense. I'm sorry to hear that."

"Don't worry, Detective," Carl said. "On my parent's death, all three of Stan's children will be cared for with trust funds and college paid."

"Three?" Lott asked.

"His wife in Winnemucca had a young girl right before he vanished, or as it turned out, was killed."

"And the other child?" Lott asked.

"My daughter," Julia said, looking at Lott with a puzzled look. "She was born three months after Stan was killed."

Lott looked at her, his mouth open.

"You're kidding?" Julia asked, now starting to suddenly get worried. "I didn't tell you I was pregnant with my daughter Jane when Stan was killed?"

Lott shook his head.

"I'm very sorry," Julia said to Lott, suddenly worried about how he would feel. "She's majoring in biochemistry at UNLV. It's why I moved to Las Vegas in the first place, to be close to her. She's so busy, we seldom talk. Not sure why I never mentioned her."

Then Julia turned back to look at Carl. "I am sure she will appreciate anything coming from her father's family, since she never knew him. But there is no need. She's doing fine with scholarships in the meantime. That's not why we are here. We want to find out who killed Stan."

Lott said nothing.

"I understand," Carl said, nodding.

Julia really hoped her surprise hadn't hurt what she was starting to enjoy with Lott. The subject of her daughter had just never come up. She hadn't been hiding it. Or at least she didn't think she had.

Dammit all to hell. What a stupid oversight on her part. She was proud of her daughter, just as he was proud of Annie.

She and Lott would have to talk when this was over. She really wanted what they were building to continue. She enjoyed his company far, far more than she wanted to admit at times.

Also, she wasn't looking forward to letting her daughter know she had a half-brother and a half-sister. That was a task she had been avoiding since they had talked to Denise.

When they got back, it was time to have that conversation as well.

CHAPTER EIGHTEEN

October, 2014
Foothills
Boise, Idaho

Lott had been shocked at learning about Julia's daughter. He had to admit that. She clearly was proud of her daughter, and clearly hadn't been hiding her from him in any fashion. It had just never come up.

And that worried him because he was really starting to fall for this woman and he realized he knew almost nothing about her. After all the years with Carol, knowing everything there was to know about Carol, he guessed he just sort of figured he would automatically know a person he was attracted to.

But that was clearly not the case. A very dumb assumption on his part.

She looked worried about him not knowing about her daughter. Clearly she also was concerned about something getting in the way of what was growing between them.

Well, as far as he was concerned, it wouldn't. He just needed to adjust his thinking some and enjoy getting to really know another person. Something he hadn't done since he and Carol had met back when he was still a traffic cop.

"So," Lott said, deciding to focus back on Carl while they had him trapped in the car. "What happened to your brother's corporation?"

Now it was Carl's turn to act surprised. "What corporation? Except for the money my parents sent him to live and an old Impala, he had nothing more than the clothes on his back."

Rogers looked at Lott and he nodded. She reached into a folder beside her on the back seat and pulled out all the information they knew about Stan's business. And with luck, Annie and Doc and Fleet would be digging up even more in the next day or so.

She handed the paper to Carl who studied it, clearly shocked. Lott had watched a lot of people pretend to be shocked. This was real.

Carl really, really hadn't known his brother ran such a large business. Rocha really had a way with secrets, that's for sure.

After a moment, Carl looked up. "Breyfogle Incorporated?"

Lott nodded. "Named after a famous lost mine to the west of Las Vegas. Your brother's company bought up land, mineral rights, and water rights all over Nevada, almost always where there was a rumored hidden treasure."

"Plus they owned three warehouses in Reno and a dozen in Las Vegas," Rogers said. "His body was found in one of the warehouses his company owned."

"We didn't know he owned the building at the time," Lott said. "We only discovered all this just lately in this new investigation."

"So what happened to all this after his death?" Carl asked,

frowning as he continued to study the paper with all the assets of the corporation listed that had been found so far. "There was a lot of money here."

"That's what we just asked you," Lott said. "We have people tracing this, but so far we have run into a dead end. Whatever happened to this corporation was very, very carefully covered up. And, of course, Nevada corporation laws make that fairly easy to do."

"This isn't possible," Carl said. "My brother was a free spirit. Smart as they came, yes, but not the corporation type. And I have no idea where he would have gotten the money for all this."

"Parents didn't fund him in any way?" Rogers asked.

"No," Carl said, shaking his head. "I'm five years older than Stan and was already doing the family books and accounting when he left college. I did the books both for our family corporations and my parent's personal money. I know of every dollar they sent him. And it wasn't much. Not enough to start this."

Carl waved around the paper and then handed it back to Rogers who put it back in the file folder.

"Did Stan have any friends in college that could have helped him with his treasure hunting?" Rogers asked.

That was a good question that Lott hadn't thought of.

Carl shook his head. "He was a loner. He had a girlfriend for the last couple years of college, but he told me she wanted to get married and he wanted to go search for lost treasure."

"A woman he didn't marry," Rogers said, laughing.

"Yeah, wondered about that after he started into marrying all of you," Carl said, shaking his head. "He did all that marrying in one year. 1988."

"When did he leave college?" Lott asked.

"1986 was when he graduated," Carl said.

"The corporation was incorporated in late 1989," Rogers said. "And started buying land shortly after."

Suddenly Lott had a thought, one that Stan's brother and Rogers weren't going to like much if he was right.

"So I assume," Lott said, "that when Stan came home, he stayed here with your parents."

Carl looked puzzled. "Stan never came home. Not once from the time he left to go treasure hunting."

Rogers jerked and looked at Lott.

"Tell me," Rogers said, "was his college girlfriend rich?"

Carl nodded, looking puzzled because he seemed to know he had missed something. "Very. Why?"

"And she had access to money, even being young?"

"I think so, why?" Carl asked. "She had a huge trust fund that she came into when she graduated. You think she funded up Stan?"

Rogers nodded. "I can't imagine the man I married saying no to a woman."

"Shit," Carl said, almost shouting. "Are you saying he might have married her as well?"

"Maybe," Lott said, keeping his voice calm. "Not a word to anyone. Let us investigate because she might be our suspect."

Carl nodded.

"Can you get us her name and address?" Rogers asked.

"I know it very well," he said, shaking his head. "Her name is Kate McDonald. She's married to the governor of the state. The Governor's Mansion is down in the north end of town. Tough to miss."

All Lott could do was stare at Carl. He didn't have one thought in his head.

Finally he glanced back at Rogers, who was also just staring blankly at Carl.

Neither of them had a thing to say.

Stan's possible first wife, possible backer in his corporation, and possible suspect in his death was a governor's wife.

They were suddenly so far in over their heads, it wasn't funny.

CHAPTER NINETEEN

October, 2014
Foothills
Boise, Idaho

Julia sat in silence as Lott drove them back off the twisting roads of the foothills and down into the tree-lined streets of the North End part of the city. She had never been in this part of the town before, and it was beautiful. Older homes tucked back from the street covered like a tunnel with branches of large oaks lining both sides.

It was shaded and cool and everything was bright green and the homes were older, but well-kept and clearly loved.

Finally she turned to Lott. "Sorry about not telling you about Jane. I'm very proud of her and can't imagine how I didn't blab about her all the time over the last week."

Lott laughed. "Shocked for a moment, but it's understandable. We've sort of been focused on figuring out who killed her father."

"But I am sorry," she said.

"Part of getting to know each other," he said, waving her apology away.

"I like getting to know you," she said, smiling at him, relieved he wasn't upset in any way. In fact, she felt more relieved than she wanted to admit. In a very short time she had really come to value and enjoy and trust Lott. And had hopes for a lot more time together if she didn't do something stupid to blow it all up.

"I like getting to know you as well," he said, giving her that smile she was really starting to love. "I have a hunch that by the time this is over, we're going to know each other a lot more."

"I hope so," she said, turning back to watch the beautiful streets and homes go past.

"I hope so as well," he said.

They rode in a comfortable and relieved silence for a few blocks down the beautiful shady streets.

"Got any ideas of what we should do next?" he asked.

"Find someplace to eat and call Andor and fill him in on all this," she said. "Before Carl calls the first wife."

"You think he might?" Lott asked.

"It's big money and politics," she said. "So come to think of it, let's do a surprise visit before she can lawyer up."

Lott glanced at her and then smiled. "That's totally crazy, but I like how you think, Detective."

It was totally crazy. She knew that, but it might be the only way they get any information at all from a governor's wife. If it wasn't already too late.

She sat back as Lott used the GPS feature in the car to direct them to the Governor's Mansion.

The big white mansion was two stories tall in this same area of town. It was tucked back in the trees with a large fence around it and surrounded by trees. It looked more like a southern home than one for Idaho.

The building didn't look much bigger than some of the other large homes nearby. But Julia could imagine back when it was first built, the mansion sat up on a slight hill looking at the valley. Now the huge old trees blocked any chance at a view.

They pulled into an area labeled guest parking just off the street and a good hundred yards from the main house across a tree-covered huge lawn. There were no other cars at this point in the early afternoon.

And no one in sight.

Julie glanced around, thinking that fact very odd.

She and Lott climbed out into the warm afternoon air and moved to the gate and the speaker there. The gate was black iron and decorative and wide enough for large trucks to pass. The rest of the fence looked about the same but was mostly covered in climbing vines. Julia could see a number of obvious security cameras and more than likely there were a few not so obvious.

One camera was mounted right over the speaker.

Lott pushed the button and a moment later a woman's voice said, "Yes."

"Las Vegas Detectives Lott and Rogers," Lott said, "to see Mrs. McDonald on a private matter."

"One moment," the voice said.

After about thirty seconds a man's voice came back. "Please show your badges to the camera."

They both did.

The gate clicked and opened. "Please come up the driveway to the security building on the left. Be prepared to leave your guns."

Lott nodded and Julia led the way through the gate. Then

the two of them moved up the beautiful flower-lined driveway. She wasn't sure what the low gold and red flowers were, but they seemed to be doing fine in the early fall heat.

Everything about this city had a beauty about it. She had never seen a place like it before. Nevada cities like Reno and Las Vegas were stark and dry, and even though Reno had the mountains towering over it, the poverty that ran alongside the casino lights was always in sharp contrast.

Here, this town seemed like the poster city for middle and upper class blue-collar living. Everything seemed maintained and painted and in the city brown didn't seem to be a color that was allowed.

At the security building, they were met by a man with a badge and a gun on his hip. Clearly in shape and more than likely military of some sort, even though he was dressed in a black shirt and black slacks and black shoes.

He checked their badges again and asked them for their guns.

"You two are a way out of jurisdiction," he said. "And retired. May I ask your business with the governor's wife?"

Julia was surprised he had discovered they were retired, but a quick internet search of the Nevada police data base would show that clearly. But it would also show their special exemption to work.

"It's a private matter involving a friend from her college days," Lott said.

Julia had no doubt that the governor's wife was watching on one of the cameras. So she decided to put her at ease a little bit. "We are working a very cold case and could use some more background information, if she wouldn't mind. We won't be long."

"Follow me," the man said, nodding after a moment.

Julia knew that more than likely the governor's wife had told him to bring them in. It was the correct political move. If she lawyered up now, it would just prove she had something to hide and that was the last thing she would want.

Their surprise visit was paying off in at least that little way. Now it would be interesting to see what kind of answers she gave them.

They were shown into a side door and into a large, high-ceiling parlor that was furnished with modern furniture. The walls were painted off-white and pictures of former governors covered two walls. Tall windows looking out over the lawn filled the other two walls.

As they entered, a woman dressed in jogging clothes and tennis shoes came in. "Sorry for the attire," she said, smiling. "You caught me in the exercise room."

She had her dark brown hair pulled back off her face and clearly she had spent time in the sun, as well as had a couple face-lifts that made her look both fake and younger at the same time.

"Very sorry to intrude," Lott said after introducing them both.

"Call me Kate, please," she said and indicated that they sit down on the couch and she sat facing them in a big chair.

"We're here in Boise investigating a cold case from Las Vegas," Julia said, starting off. "Stan Rocha was murdered in 1992 and his murder never solved."

Kate nodded. "I know," she said. "I'm glad you are opening it back up finally."

"How do you know about the murder?" Julia asked.

"Stan was my first husband," Kate said, looking Julia right in the eye.

Julia nodded. So they had been right after all.

"When Stan didn't come home," Kate said, "I sent investigators to find him. About six months after his death they discovered he had been shot in Las Vegas. It barely even made the papers at the time since there were no leads and so many other more important things happening in Las Vegas at the time."

"Is that when you discovered your first husband's habits with other women?" Lott said.

Kate didn't even bat an eye. "No, actually. Stan told me about all of his other wives in 1989, after he had married them all, including you, Detective Rogers."

Julia sat back. This was not going the way she had expected. Not at all.

"So you were angry?" Lott asked.

Kate actually laughed. "Not in the slightest. I forced him into marrying me after all. Poor Stan could never say no to a woman on anything."

Then Kate turned. "He liked you the most of all of them," she said.

Julie had no idea at all how to answer that, so she only nodded.

"Did you know about his three children?" Lott asked.

"Five children," she said. "I had two children with him as well. Both now grown and married and doing well."

"So your past with Stan is known?" Julia asked, trying to ignore for the moment the thought of now telling Jane she had four half-brothers and sisters.

Kate actually laughed at that. "Of course. You don't be married to a man running for any political office and try to hide things like this. The press knows I was married before Madison and had two children and that my first husband was killed in Las Vegas. And that his murder is unsolved."

Kate took a deep breath, clearly lost in memory. "Madison

stepped in and helped when Stan vanished and did a great job being a father to my two children after we learned of Stan's death. The children were both so young, they don't remember their real father at all."

"He knew you before Stan was killed?" Lott asked.

Kate smiled. "There were five of us who hung around together in college. Me and Stan and Madison and Carla and Danny. Great friends."

Julia nodded. Clearly Stan's brother didn't know about any of this with his younger brother, including the two kids, so this kind of thing wasn't in the news much. Although from what she could tell of Stan's older brother, he didn't pay much attention to anything but his parents and his family money.

"One more question if you don't mind," Lott asked.

Kate waved her hand. "Glad to help, detectives, if it solves Stan's murder. And besides, you are helping me avoid a long half hour on the StairMaster."

"Did you know about his corporation?" Lott asked.

Julia was watching Kate closely when he asked that question and she was honestly shocked.

"What corporation?" Kate asked, leaning forward. "Stan had no money, which is why he married in every town, to have a place to stay while he searched for his lost treasures. I wouldn't give him any of my trust fund's money. I told him that was for the kids and to buy us all a house when he got done with his treasure quest, since he wasn't actually working. And my parents were disgusted I had married him and wouldn't talk with me for years, even after Stan's death became known."

Lott shook his head and Julia did the same.

"What corporation?" Kate asked again, this time in a powerful, demanding voice that Julia instantly understood why Stan couldn't say no to her.

"Stan was the president and CEO and only officer of record in a Nevada Corporation called Breyfogle Incorporated," Lott said, "named after a lost mine to the west of Las Vegas."

"It was founded in 1986," Julia said, "and had property, mineral rights, and water rights all over the state, mostly corresponding with the areas of old lost mines and treasures. We only just learned about it."

"And it owned almost a dozen major warehouses," Lott said, including the one where his body was found. We just learned that as well."

Kate looked like she had lost most of her dark tan as she sat back in the big chair. "That's not possible."

"What's not possible," Julia said.

"Stan called me all excited one day that he had found one of his lost mines," Kate said. "He had done that maybe a dozen times before, usually to beg me to send him some money. I always refused and just ignored him on that call. But that time he didn't ask for money, and since I was pregnant with our second child, I didn't think much about it."

Lott glanced at Julia, then leaned forward. "Are you saying you think he might have actually found one of the lost treasures and not told you?"

Kate took a deep breath and leaned forward, clearly gathering herself. She looked at Julia. "You were married to him, Detective. Could he have kept that from you?"

"I didn't even know he was searching for treasure," Julia said, smiling. "Stan was the most tightlipped person I have ever met and the deeper I get into this investigation, the more I understand I knew nothing about the man I married and had a child with."

"Well," Kate said, sitting back and closing her eyes. "It seems that makes two of us."

CHAPTER TWENTY

October, 2014
Downtown
Boise, Idaho

Lott drove in silence through the beautiful, oak-covered streets of the North End of Boise, Idaho, heading back toward the center part of town. He knew where there was a decent restaurant down near the city parks on the river where they could have a late lunch. He was starving.

"It's been a long time since crawling out of bed this morning in Las Vegas," Rogers said, smiling at him. "I feel sort of shell-shocked to be honest."

"Food will help," Lott said.

"Soon, I hope," Rogers said.

"As fast as I can get us there without getting arrested."

She laughed.

They rode in silence for a few more blocks, then Rogers said, "We have five wives, five kids, a brother who is as much in the dark as anyone, and a lost corporation. That guy I married was a real piece of work, wasn't he?"

"He had his issues," Lott said, smiling at Rogers. "But if he did find that lost gold mine, how he dealt with it was far from stupid. He kept it out of the papers and kept the money to himself."

Suddenly Rogers turned toward him. "Gold mine," she said. "If he did find a gold mine, someone would have to work it. Right?"

Lott nodded, starting to see where she was headed.

"The ore would have to be processed and sold," she said, "and there would be records of all that in the state records. Right?"

"I know nothing about gold mining," Lott said, "but I'm betting you are on the money about that."

"We get to the restaurant," she said, "we have to call Andor and fill him in on all this."

"And we need to get Annie and Doc and their people looking into the mining of the Breyfogle as well," Lott said.

"Every time we hit a dead end on this, another five leads spring up," Rogers said.

"It certainly is keeping it interesting," Lott said, feeling both frustrated and challenged. It really felt good to be working on a case like this. His retirement had been clouded with Carol's sickness and death. He knew he hadn't been ready to retire and now it felt great to be back.

"If I don't get some food pretty soon," Rogers said, smiling at him, "I might make this case even more interesting by passing out on you."

"Six blocks," Lott said, turning on Capital Boulevard toward the old Union Pacific Historical Train Station on the hill. The place was the subject of just about half the postcards that came out of Boise. And he had to admit, driving toward it, the big clock tower and sprawling grounds around the building on the hill did make it look like a postcard.

The restaurant he was aiming for was in a building just over the bridge and close to the edge of Boise State University. A steakhouse with huge sandwiches and perfect iced tea. Annie and Doc had brought him here on his only visit up to see them and he had wanted to go back ever since.

He pulled into the mostly empty parking lot and they headed through the warm afternoon air toward the front door of the red-brick exterior tucked in under some tall pine and fir trees. There was a smell of freshly-mowed grass combining with the smell of cooking steak. Just about perfect for an early fall afternoon.

Inside, the steak smell got stronger and Lott could feel his stomach starting to really rumble and his mouth watering. A waitress with brown hair and a matching brown uniform with tan blouse and brown slacks and shoes got them seated at a big wooden table with soft booth seats around it. The seats were made out of some fake leather but were amazingly comfortable.

"Do you have some sort of bread we could snack on while we look at the menu?" Lott asked.

"Crazy hungry," Rogers said, smiling at the waitress who smiled back and promised to bring their classic butter rolls with their two iced teas.

Lot glanced at her. "You get Andor, I'll call Annie and get her started on the research on the mine."

"You got it," she said.

They were both talking when the waitress got back with the drinks and bread. And they both stopped the conversation long enough to take a large bite of the butter roll. It tasted like heaven as far as he was concerned.

Across the table, Rogers rolled her eyes in pleasure as she bit into the roll and all he could do was laugh. He was really enjoying his time with her. He had to trust that if they did solve this case, their time together would continue.

For some reason, he had just thought himself too old to get romantically involved again. And too set in his ways, as Carol had often said of him.

But it seems Rogers wasn't giving him much choice in the matter. If she just wasn't so damn good-looking and funny and smart and fun to be with, he might be able to stop the feelings.

But she was all of those things and he was going to have to relax and just go with it.

Far, far easier said than done.

CHAPTER TWENTY-ONE

October, 2014
Downtown
Boise, Idaho

Lott explained to his daughter, Annie, what had happened with the brother and then at the Governor's Mansion. Annie had been flat stunned that they had had the courage to just go investigate the governor's wife.

Lott mentioned that if Annie had people doing research, it would be helpful to see if there were any articles on the governor's wife's first marriage when he was running for office.

And articles about the two kids.

Annie said she was excited to be involved and said she would get people on that, on the mining output, and permits and everything. So far they had found no further trace of what happened to who controlled the corporation after Rocha was killed.

Rogers finished her conversation with Andor just slightly before Lott hung up with his daughter.

"He thinks we were nuts," she said, smiling as she took out another roll.

"Annie thought the same thing. But I have her investigating the governor's wife's story. And her kids."

"Good," Rogers said. "And you have her going on the mineral sales from a mine like the Breyfogle."

"I do," Lott said.

"Andor's still searching for the Impala," Rogers said. "Trying to figure out who owned it. He checked if Rocha had registered it in Idaho, but he hadn't. Andor will look into the chance that the governor's wife had owned it."

"Oh, great thinking," he said as the waitress came with her order pad and another basket of hot butter rolls that seemed to melt in his mouth.

They both ordered steaks and baked potatoes. He ordered a rib-eye and she ordered a top sirloin, both medium rare.

Then as the waitress left, they both grabbed a hot roll. The food was helping him, and from what he could tell, Rogers was feeling better as well.

"So what's next on our plan?" he asked.

She opened her notebook and looked at her notes. "We've talked to the brother and he didn't even know his brother was ever in town or about his first wife."

"And the first wife was shocked by the news of the corporation and possible mine," Lott said.

"She was," Rogers said, nodding and staring at her notebook.

Lott watched her, trying to figure out what was bothering him. Something pretty major, but he just couldn't put his finger on it.

"We need to investigate the two friends the governor's wife mentioned," Rogers said after a moment.

Rogers nodded and then what had been bothering him suddenly snapped into place. "Who would have the power to hide a corporation and even help Stan set it up?"

"Someone with money," Rogers said, frowning.

"Exactly," Lott said. "We need to have a look at the governor's early days. Did he have money? Was he the backer behind his friend's crazy searches?"

"Love triangle," Rogers said, nodding. "I'll bet he was in love with Kate and helped Stan leave to search for treasure to try to work his way into Kate's life."

"It makes as much sense as anything we've come up with so far," Lott said. "I'll call Annie and get her researching into McDonald's past as well."

Rogers nodded and looked at her notes again. "We're still missing one major thing we came looking for. Where did he keep his extra stuff, his driver's licenses, corporate records, things like that?"

Lott finished off the last of the roll as he thought about that. She was right. Rocha's mother didn't have any of it. The governor's wife clearly didn't have it since, if she had, she would have known about the corporation.

"So we have a missing corporation and a missing stash of personal papers," Lott said. "Wouldn't surprise me that McDonald had it all."

"It would make sense," Rogers said. "But it made sense his mother had it all."

"True," Lott said. So far this case was just one crazy twist and turn and dead-end road after another.

"We're also missing a car," Rogers said.

"Seems that while everyone is digging into the past, we need to talk to the other two wives. Maybe he confided in one of them."

Rogers nodded and put her notebook away as the waitress brought their food. "I was afraid you were going to say that."

"You want me to go?" Lott asked, studying her.

She shook her head. "I've met two of them. I can manage the other two. And we're making a great team talking with them."

He smiled. "That we are."

Then, before he dug into his wonderful-smelling steak and baked potato, he called Annie back.

After he quickly told her what they thought might have happened with the love triangle and the governor, all she said was, "What a hornet's nest."

"Just have your investigator be very careful," Lott said.

Annie actually laughed at that. "Oh, trust me, no trace. Our people are that good. Just you two don't kick the thing anymore."

"I promise," he said.

His daughter just laughed at him, knowing that he was just joking.

He hung up and dug into his steak. Across the table Rogers was already halfway done with hers.

And smiling with every bite.

CHAPTER TWENTY-TWO

October, 2014
Boise Airport
Boise, Idaho

Julia stood just inside the air-conditioned private building that served as the office and waiting room for Doc Hill's private jet. The room was carpeted and had three expensive couches and a couple of magazines on a coffee table. Against one wall was a coffee and tea bar and some fresh doughnuts filled a plate there as well.

If she hadn't been so full from the wonderful steak dinner, she would have taken one.

The ground crew had just finished up a flight check and now they were all waiting for a copilot to arrive. Then she and Lott would be headed out.

She couldn't believe, and never would have believed, that on any case as a detective, she would be flying in such comfort and style.

Yet here she stood, waiting a few minutes for people to service a private jet just for her and Lott to fly to Winnemucca and then on to Salt Lake so they could talk to her former husband's other wives.

Actually, she more than likely should stop thinking of Stan as her former husband. Their marriage had never been valid, since he had already been married before her to at least one other woman. It had been a sham from moment one.

She still couldn't believe that she had missed the signs that Stan wasn't what he seemed. As a detective, she had always prided herself in catching the smallest details in a case. She had always figured that Stan might have a girlfriend somewhere, but since she didn't really even know what he did when he left and couldn't get him to talk about it at all, she clearly hadn't cared that much.

Something about that bothered her as well. Maybe she knew, deep down, that she was only a rest stop for Stan to drop by at times and have sex and eat and sleep. And the marriage had just made it seem right to her for a time.

Looking back, she didn't think she much cared at all until she got pregnant with Jane.

Julia shook that thought away. Once they found Stan's killer, she was going to search out a counselor and get some help putting all this in perspective. Just so she could safely trust herself with another relationship.

She glanced back at the small waiting area. Lott was pacing in front of one couch, talking with his daughter. Maybe Annie and her research team had found something.

She hoped so.

It had been a very long day since she and Lott had climbed on that plane in Las Vegas a little before eight in the morning. Now it was going on six in the evening Boise time. Once they were in the air, they would be in Winnemucca in thirty minutes. They hoped to talk with the wife there and be back in the air and on the way to Salt Lake in an hour.

Through the big window, Julia could see a man dressed like a pilot walk toward the plane and climb on board. Looks like they were about ready.

"Talk to you after we talk with the Winnemucca wife," Lott said to his daughter and clicked off the phone.

"Any luck," Julia asked as he came over to stand beside her.

"The Breyfogle Company and the sole stock owner were extremely rich," Lott said. "Annie thinks they are getting closer to digging out who that person is."

"Mining money?" Julia asked.

"Gold and silver," Lott said. "Plus plowing the money into more land and water rights and mineral rights made them even richer very quickly. Annie and her people are finding that information out easily enough, just not who was running the place."

"How about employee names," Julia asked.

Lott nodded. "They've got about fifty higher level manager's names, some of which were vice presidents. If we need to, we can interview them."

Julia knew that would be a lot of work, but if they hit solid dead-ends from here, they would do just that.

"Governor was broke as a college student," Lott said. "He had no real money until he married Kate. It seemed her family approved of him."

"Any chance Kate's family might have a hand in Stan's murder?" Julia asked.

"A logical motive," Lott said. "Annie and her people are digging into them all. Bound to be some ugly rat's nests back in those lives somewhere."

"You mean more ugly than a governor's wife being married to a bigamist before she married the governor?"

Lott laughed. "Seems that detail never hit any papers."

"Yet," Julia said.

From the door of the jet, Julia saw the pilot wave for them to come out.

"Well, you ready to go talk with one of your husband's other wives?" Lott asked as they headed out the door and into the warm evening air and the rumbling noises of the airport around them.

"You sure know how to make a trip sound exciting," Julia said.

"Better than Disneyland," Lott said.

"Wifeland?" Julia asked. "We find many more wives and it just might be enough for a theme park."

Lott laughed. "And all the kids could run it."

Julia really laughed. "Got that right. I'm not looking forward to telling Jane she has four half-brothers and sisters."

"Don't blame you there at all," Lott said, now suddenly serious as they neared the plane. "Might want to talk with Annie about that problem before you talk to Jane. Get a younger person's perspective on how to approach it."

Lott stopped at the bottom of the stairs leading up into the jet and looked at her directly, those wonderful dark eyes of his clearly worried about her.

"I will," she said, smiling at him. "Thanks. And thanks for the great dinner."

And then she did something that surprised even herself.

She kissed him lightly on the lips before starting up the stairs. Sort of a thank-you kiss and a promise of the future kiss.

And it was nice. Really nice, especially the totally surprised look on his face as she turned away.

CHAPTER TWENTY-THREE

October, 2014
Winnemucca, Nevada

From the air, as the jet turned to make an approach to the runway, Winnemucca wasn't much more than a wide area of buildings and some casino signs stretching along the old highway beside the freeway between Reno and Salt Lake. The town had been there long before the freeway, and parts of it showed, even from a couple thousand feet in the air.

The town had spread out some with some classic subdivisions and mobile home parks on the road toward Boise. The desert around it was brown and there weren't many patches of green showing at all. Very, very different from the city of Boise, where everything seemed green and covered by lush trees.

Somehow, Annie had arranged for them to have a car waiting. Lott was pretty convinced that Doc had called in a favor from a local casino owner who had sent a minion to rent a car and wait at the airport.

They weren't going to have the car more than an hour if everything went as planned.

He and Julia had talked about the case on the way down, both puzzling about how Stan had managed to start the corporation and keep it secret from all his wives.

Not a word was said about the kiss getting into the plane. Lott had been shocked. He had to admit that. But not upset. He hoped at some point to be kissing-close to Julia and it appeared she hoped the same thing about him.

They had called ahead from Boise to the Winnemucca wife whose actual name was Stephanie Benz. She was a bookkeeper and her husband owned a small restaurant near one end of town that geared mostly to the locals instead of the tourists coming through.

She had agreed to talk with them when she learned it was about Stan Rocha. She said her husband was at work and it would be better if they could meet her at her office in the back of a service station and repair shop.

Lott had little doubt that the woman would add anything to the picture they were building, but they didn't dare not talk with her and let her know what was happening. And that her daughter had grandparents in Boise that were very rich.

Since Stan's brother had known about the kids and done nothing to help in their support, Lott was hoping that some of the wives just might go after the family. He knew Rogers never would, and he knew Kate, the wife of the governor, didn't need to. But the other three certainly could make Carl pay a little for his cold heartedness over the years in not helping out with his brother's children.

Stephanie turned out to be another thin, blonde, smoker, with a smoker's cough and rough voice. She sort of reminded Lott of Denise Miller in Las Vegas.

Stephanie's office was stacked high with files and a full ashtray the size of a dinner plate dominated one corner of her desk.

"Can we talk outside?" Lott asked, after they were introduced. He had no desire to smell like a dead ashtray all the way to Salt Lake.

"Thank you," Rogers whispered to him as she went past him back out into the fresh, desert air that smelled of hot sagebrush instead of a full ashtray.

Stephanie didn't seem to mind and as soon as they were outside on the parking area in the shade of the building, she lit up another Camel.

"So what did you find out about Stan?" she asked after blowing the smoke up into the warm evening air.

"He was killed in Las Vegas in 1992," Lott said, letting Rogers just take notes.

"Figured something like that happened to him," she said. "He learned I was pregnant and just vanished into thin air. I got the marriage annulled three years later and married Burt. We had two more kids and he treated Stan's kid like his own."

"Nice of him," Rogers said, writing on her notepad while talking.

"So why are you here after all these years?" Stephanie asked.

"We're trying to find out who killed him," Rogers said. "You have any idea who might have wanted him dead?"

Stephanie laughed and then coughed. "Stan was a mooch, but a nice guy. Can't imagine why anyone would want him dead."

"You know what he did for a living?" Lott asked.

"Some sort of traveling salesman I figured," she said. "He never told me. Then she looked puzzled. "When did you say he was killed?"

"May 1992," Lott said, glancing at Rogers who had a puzzled look on her face.

"Weird," Stephanie said, blowing smoke out her nose as she said that. "He must have joined Elvis and his crew."

"What do you mean?" Rogers asked.

"Oh, people around town said they spotted him at times over the next ten years, mostly out along the highway headed south. I just figured they were either imagining things, or Stan didn't want to see me anymore because I had a kid. I was always pissed at him for not stopping and seeing his kid."

She laughed again. "Guess he couldn't do that, being dead and all."

"Yeah, kind of tough," Lott said, shaking his head.

Rogers smiled at him and they asked Stephanie a few more basic questions, then gave her Carl's address in Boise and headed back for the airport.

"You doing okay?" Lott asked Rogers. He was really worried about her and this entire task of telling Stan's other wives what had happened.

"Actually doing fine," Rogers said, smiling at him with that wonderful smile of hers. "And thanks for getting us out of that office."

"I think we lost some years off our lives just stepping in there," Lott said.

"I still think that once we are back at the plane I'm going to change clothes."

Lott nodded to that. They had both brought along overnight bags just in case they were forced to stay in Boise. But now it was possible they could talk to the Salt Lake wife and be home for a late meal at the Bellagio and then a regular night's sleep. They might as well get out of the smoke residue for the next part of the trip.

"So what did you think of that?" Lott asked her as they pulled in near the plane at the small airport runway. They had only been away from the plane for less than thirty minutes.

"I liked that she thought Stan joined Elvis," Rogers said, shaking her head.

Lott laughed, but he suddenly had an idea that none of them had yet considered.

As Rogers was in the back private area of the plane changing clothes, he called Annie.

"Did Rocha's company have any mining operations to the south of Winnemucca?"

"Hang on," she said and he could hear some rustling of papers.

"Yeah, he did," she said. "An old lost silver mine about thirty miles south. Company bought the land in 1993 and opened up a mine there in 1995. Why?"

"Because the Winnemucca wife said there were sightings of Stan like Elvis years after he was killed. All south of town."

"Now that's weird," Annie said. "You sure that was Rocha's body you found?"

"We were at the time," Lott said. "Thanks, I'll call Andor and get him on it first thing in the morning."

"I'll keep that angle in mind as well."

He had just got Andor to pick up the phone when Rogers came out of the back wearing a clean white blouse and tan slacks. Her hair was brushed back and tied and her face looked like it was freshly washed.

She was amazingly attractive.

"You remember," Lott said to Andor, "how we confirmed the identity of the body?"

Across from him Rogers' eyes got huge.

"Clothes, driver's license on the body was about it if I remember right."

"That's what I remember as well," Lott said.

"You saying that might have been someone else?"

"This case is so strange, I don't think we can rule out anything."

"I agree," Andor said.

Lott looked at Rogers. "You up for taking a look at the scene pictures and autopsy pictures?"

"Not a problem," she said.

"Can you have the pictures waiting for us at the airport in Salt Lake in about thirty minutes?"

"I can't," Andor said, laughing. "But I'll bet your daughter can get them right out of the computer file and fire them to you. Want me to call her?"

"Would you?" Lott asked. "We're going to be in the air shortly and she knows my suspicion."

"Where did this come from?" Andor asked.

"Elvis," Lott said, laughing. "I'll explain later. Just get that information on the way."

"Autopsy results as well," Rogers said loud enough for Andor to hear.

As Lott hung up and put his phone away, he looked at Rogers puzzled.

"He had a tattoo on his left leg. Always wondered what it meant."

"What was it?" Lott asked.

"The letters KM in bright red and blue on his hip where no one would see them unless he was naked."

Lott felt even more puzzled. "KM?"

"Kate McDonald," Rogers said. "His only real wife. I just now put that together."

"Sorry," Lott said.

She waved him off. "Just go get changed so we can get this flight in the air."

He nodded. She was as tough a detective as they came, he had no doubt about that. But he had no idea how she was standing up to all this. He doubted he'd be able to.

CHAPTER TWENTY-FOUR

October, 2014
Salt Lake City International Airport
Salt Lake, Utah

It was after eight in the evening Salt Lake time, seven Las Vegas time. Lott and Rogers sat on Doc Hill's private jet, comparing notes, trying to figure out exactly where they should go next. April had brought them both glasses of iced tea and it tasted wonderful to Lott.

It had been a long day for both of them, and Lott's feeling was that they should head back to Las Vegas as planned and get some sleep.

But they had decided to take thirty minutes and make sure of that decision before telling the pilots to go.

Plus, they were waiting for the files with the pictures from the autopsy and the warehouse to come in to make sure they were chasing the right murder.

Ruby Rocha, Stan's Salt Lake wife, turned out to be deep in

her faith when she married Stan for life and into the next life and forever, as her church believed. When he left, she had just waited for him to return.

That simple.

She had waited for twenty-two years.

She had done nothing else with her life, it seemed.

Tragic, very tragic as far as Lott was concerned. And he caught himself thinking that and wondering a little if he hadn't been doing the same thing with how he felt about Carol. More than likely, he had.

Maybe it really was time, as Annie kept telling him, to move on. He could wait until the day he died and Carol would never return. He had to finally admit that. He didn't want to, but he had to.

That fact was really hard to see when inside the feelings. Not so hard to see when looking at Ruby Rocha lying in a huge Hospice Care bed. She now weighed almost four hundred pounds and was being chewed up by all the problems associated with not taking care of herself medically at that weight. Plus she had a couple forms of cancer that had gone untreated.

They found her in an assisted living home and the nurse on duty had warned them to not upset her. She had very little time left to live. Maybe less than a month.

So they had decided to just not talk with her. There seemed to be no point. Stan Rocha, by marrying her, had killed Ruby just as effectively as putting a bullet in her brain.

So they had headed back to the airport, riding in silence in the cab they had decided to take to see Ruby. It seemed neither of them wanted to talk about her. Lott knew he sure didn't.

There just wasn't much to talk about.

By the time they got back in the plane, the files had not yet arrived from Annie with Stan's autopsy pictures. So they sat across from each other in big leather chairs, their notebooks in hand, iced teas beside them, going back over everything from the day.

Lott had no idea how much this jet cost Doc, but Lott sure liked the comfort of it.

They had just finished when the pilot, a smiling young man by the name of Lawrence, wearing dark slacks and a white dress shirt with his sleeves rolled up, came back into the cabin and said, "Detectives, the information you are waiting for from Annie is coming through now."

He pointed to a desk in the rear of the main cabin, tucked off to the right side. He went to it and pushed a couple of buttons and a monitor rose from the desk and a keyboard swung out.

Lott just shook his head. Of course a private plane like this would have a desk to work at, just as it had a bedroom in the back to sleep in.

Lawrence got the computer up and running for them with a couple more buttons and then said, "Let me know when you are ready to go. And to where."

"Thanks," Lott said. "Really appreciate it."

The pilot nodded. "Glad to help out." He then headed back toward the front as Julia sat down at the screen and pulled up the images.

Lott stood over her right shoulder so he could see the screen as well. He hoped this was a good idea. He knew Rogers was a good detective and had seen her share of death scenes, but seeing her own husband the way they had found him wasn't going to be easy.

The first one was of the warehouse scene and it made Julia sit back slightly.

It actually surprised Lott a little as well. He hadn't looked at those pictures for a long time. There was a bloated man's body in pants and a ripped-open shirt lying face-up on the floor, dead eyes staring at the ceiling.

The image brought back the incredible memories of that case for Lott, mostly attached to the smell of that body being in a hot warehouse and on the floor for seven days before being found.

It was not a smell he ever wanted to remember. No human death smell ever was. It was the kind of cloying, thick smell that ate at you and got into every pore of your skin and clothes. Carol hadn't let him anywhere near the insides of the house when he got home that day. She had forced him to take his clothes off in the garage and then run for the shower while she opened windows.

It had taken a week for the smell to be completely out of his car after the short ride home. He had finally had to take the car in and have it detailed out to get rid of the last of it.

And Carol did something with his clothes that involved a long stick and a big black garbage bag.

The body in the image was even more bloated than Lott remembered it being. Lott now understood why they had just assumed the wallet with the victim was the right one. They had tested the fingerprints as well, but Stan Rocha's prints had not been in the system.

"Can't tell," Julia said, shaking her head as she clicked through the five or six angles of photos of the body. "Looks like him in general. Same basic size and shape."

Then she brought up the first autopsy photo and gasped.

It was of the same bloated body, only now naked, the clothes cut away, the body lying on the morgue table.

"You all right?" he asked, putting his hand gently on her shoulder. He liked the feel of her strong muscles under his touch and he let his hand rest there only a moment before pulling it away.

"I am," she said. "But your hunch was right. That's not Stan Rocha."

Now it was Lott's turn to jerk. He had suggested that because of the Winnemucca wife's comment. He really didn't expect to be right.

"How can you be so sure?" he asked, staring at the bloated body on the table.

"He's missing the KM tattoo on his side," she said, pointing.

Lott nodded.

She clicked to the image of the other hip.

Nothing there either.

"And Stan was circumcised," Rogers said, pointing at the body's private parts.

It was very clear to Lott this man had not been circumcised in any fashion.

"I'll be go to hell," Lott said, standing and stepping back as Rogers quickly moved through the rest of the photos, then clicked off the computer and turned to him.

"So who the hell is our murder victim?" Lott asked, feeling more stunned than he wanted to admit.

"And where did Stan disappear to?" Rogers asked.

"And did he kill that man to stage his own disappearance?" Lott asked.

They both remained in silence for a moment before Lott finally broke it. "I think we need to head back to Vegas."

Julia nodded. "I agree. Stan is wrapped up in this completely, since his identity was on the body. He staged this I'm betting anything. But we need to go back and start over, look at every-thing again."

"Do you really think that the man you knew could execute someone to stage his own death?" Lott asked.

"Honestly," Rogers said, "I can't imagine Stan hurting a fly. But I can imagine him staging all this. He hid a lot from me, and his other wives, and his family. This kind of deception is right up his alley."

With that, Lott nodded and turned to the front of the plane to tell the pilots to take them home.

After that he turned back to see Julia watching him. He smiled at her. "Looks like Elvis hasn't left the building just yet."

She actually laughed.

He sat down and buckled in across from her and for the entire short flight to Las Vegas, all he could think about was how he mis-identified the victim in his very first case as a detective.

PART THREE

CHAPTER TWENTY-FIVE

October, 2014
Las Vegas International Airport
Las Vegas, Nevada

Julia was glad that Lott hadn't wanted to talk much on the trip back to Vegas. The flight had only taken less than forty minutes and the entire time she just kept going over and over what they had discovered.

The real stunner was that Stan might still be alive. How he had remained hidden for twenty-two years was beyond her, but if he was alive, he had done just that.

She had spent over two decades knowing he was dead. And Jane had always thought her father murdered. How was she going to react to all this?

Julia decided that she would wait until they had all this solved before even thinking of talking with Jane.

Also, there was something about that body in the warehouse that seemed familiar. And it wasn't because it had a general simi-

133

larity to Stan. For some reason that body and how it had been shot rang bells for her. She just couldn't, for the life of her, remember from what.

After they landed and the jet was moving toward the private hangar areas, she looked at Lott. "We got to tell Andor and Annie about this."

Lott nodded. "Thinking the same thing. Got any ideas after that?"

She shook her head. "That body looks vaguely familiar somehow, but darned if I can place it."

"It does?" Lott asked, looking puzzled. "And not because it looks like Stan?

She shook her head. "There's something else. The bullet pattern for one. Was his shirt closed or open when he was shot?"

Lott frowned. "Open. No holes in the shirt at all, and the bullets didn't go through, so no holes in the back either."

'So the body might have been dressed in Stan's clothes after it was shot."

"Likely," Lott said. "I remember that we were very frustrated because the body had been cleaned before it was dumped. No trace evidence at all except for the residue that Annie traced in her investigation."

"Weird, just damn weird," Annie said, shaking her head. There wasn't a damn thing about this case that had been straightforward.

"We'll run the prints," Lott said. "I'll have Andor do that quickly. It's only a bit after eight here."

"Feels a lot later than that," she said. "Long day."

"A productive one, though," Lott said. "You hungry?"

"I will be after a shower and a change of clothes," she said, smiling at him.

"Me too," Lott said, nodding as the plane eased to a stop.

"I'll call Annie, tell her what we discovered, and see if she can meet us at the Café Bellagio a little after nine."

"I'll call Andor," she said. "I'll get him on the fingerprints and have him meet us as well."

"We have a plan," Lott said, smiling.

Julia felt glad for at least that much.

But deep down inside, she was feeling shocked that Stan might still be alive. And that if he was alive, he had let her raise Jane alone and never helped in the slightest.

And that just pissed her off.

CHAPTER TWENTY-SIX

October, 2014
Café Bellagio
Las Vegas, Nevada

Julia felt a lot better once she had gotten home, taken a quick shower, and gotten into some fresh clothes. She needed to be comfortable tonight, so she went with a tan blouse, dark slacks, and comfortable low-heeled shoes. She pulled her hair back off her face and left it down long.

It was still a warm evening outside, but she grabbed a light jacket just in case she would need it later, and then headed for her car.

After just this one day, it was amazing how much more she knew about her former husband. Far more than she ever imagined knowing. Certainly a lot more than she knew about him when they were married.

There was a large part of her that was angry at herself. How could she not know all this back when they were together. Stan had been a master of hiding things, and she had been a master of denial. In a marriage, it always took two.

It was still going to take some time for her to forgive herself for not knowing at least some of this.

One thing for certain, as the day had gone on, she had gotten angrier and angrier at Stan. And now that she had a hunch he staged his own death, her anger was boiling. Especially after seeing what he had done to Ruby in Salt Lake. She had played the part of the dutiful wife, waiting for the missing husband to return.

And if he was alive, he had just left her.

And now that devotion was going to kill Ruby in a very ugly fashion.

Maybe, just maybe, Julia knew she might have been doing the same thing, avoiding relationships, never remarrying. And she had at least thought Stan was dead.

Why hadn't she moved on as well?

That was going to be a topic she and a counselor were going to work out as soon as they had some more answers as to what really happened to Stan.

By the time she made it to the Café Bellagio, Lott was already sitting with his daughter at a table tucked off to one side.

Annie got up, smiling and hugged Julia.

"Thank Doc for the use of his plane," Julia said as they sat down. "It was a joy to be in and allowed a lot of this to happen today."

"That it did," Lott said, nodding.

"Doc said he was just glad he could help," Annie said. "He'll join us as soon as he's done with the tournament."

Julia nodded. The daily tournaments at the Bellagio often attracted some of the top players in the world. She had stood on the rail and watched many hours of those tournaments. At some point, she hoped to have enough courage and money to sit down in one. But for the moment, when she got back to playing poker, she would keep herself satisfied playing with the tourists in some of the other rooms with buy-ins under a hundred bucks instead of north of a thousand.

"I'm dying to hear what you two found today," Annie said. "From the tidbits Dad has been giving me along the way, it was amazing amounts."

Lott smiled at his daughter. "Soon as Andor gets here, we'll lay it all out."

"He's on his way," Julia said, pointing in the direction of Andor coming in the door.

As he came up to the table, he dropped a manila file folder in front of Julia.

He nodded to everyone and then sat down.

After the day, Julia was almost afraid to pick up the folder and see what was in it.

"Rogers, you said you thought the body looked familiar," Andor said, smiling at her. "More than just a passing resemblance to your ex-husband."

"I did," Julia said. "Can't seem to get a grasp on from where though."

Andor pointed at the file. "You two just solved one of Reno's most famous missing body cases."

Suddenly she knew exactly where she recognized the body.

"The fingerprints match the Stanton Case?" she asked, staring at Andor. Was that even possible?

Andor grinned. "Spot on the money."

"I'll be go to hell," she said, opening the file to stare at naked pictures of Benny Stanton. The same guy, the same bullet patterns, only he was not bloated at all. The photo she had in front of her was taken just before an autopsy was supposed to have taken place on the body.

And just before the body vanished without a trace from the ME's basement office.

The guy who had executed Benny Stanton had already confessed, and they had the pictures and crime scene photos, so the body vanishing had just been an annoyance and a headline grabber in the papers. She remembered it well as a city cop, not yet a detective. It was the topic of a lot of conversations for months after it happened.

She couldn't remember the name of the family member who had shot Benny, but the last Julia had heard, he had died in prison a few years back. That body going missing had caused a real stir in Reno.

No one seemed to have a motive for taking it, and there were no suspects at all. It just wasn't often a body was stolen like that.

From that point forward, for years, it had always been sort of a standard joke among detectives to try to not pull "a Stanton" when they were dealing with a body.

"Someone want to fill all of us in?" Annie asked.

She turned the folder around so Lott and his daughter could see them. "We don't have a murder."

Lott looked at her, clearly puzzled.

"That's Benny Stanton," Julia said, feeling amazingly light and happy at the moment. "He was shot and killed by a family member in a fight over a car twenty-two years ago. The family member confessed and died in prison. Benny's body was stolen from the ME's office right before the autopsy was to be performed. No trace, no motive, nothing."

"So you're telling us that Stan Rocha wasn't killed back then?" Annie asked, looking up at her.

"That's right," Julia said. "My gut tells me that Stan stole Benny's body, dressed it in his clothes, left his wallet with it, and then put it in a warehouse where eventually someone would find it."

"And he would be declared dead," Lott said.

"Exactly," Julia said.

"And what happened to Stan?" Andor asked. "With five wives and five kids, I can sort of see why he would want to vanish. But where'd he go?"

Julie looked over at Annie, who was smiling at that question. Julia had a hunch Annie knew the answer, but she wanted to let Annie confirm it.

"He just kept running his company," Annie said. "He never went anywhere. A man by the name of David Buel, ran the companies. It wasn't until we went back into the history of the Lost Breyfogle Mine legend that we ran across the name of David Buel. Breyfogle worked for a David Buel back in the 1870s."

"You're kidding me?" Andor asked.

"Nope," Annie said.

Julia nodded. "The minute I realized he wasn't killed, I knew he had to have kept working, chasing his lost mines. Tell me, did that company of his have any money?"

"Not a penny," Annie said, taking a file from the floor beside her chair and sliding it over to Julia. "Every dollar it earned it sank back into buying more property and land and mining rights. Land rich, cash very poor. In fact, it had no employees, even though we thought it did at first. That's why it was so hard to track. Buel was the only name associated with the company at all."

"So the son-of-a-bitch really was broke when we were together," Julia said, nodding. "Did he make any money on the sale?"

"From what my people can find," Annie said, "he made a lot. But it was structured to pay out over a ten-year period, the last year being next year."

Julia looked at Lott, then at Andor, who was looking as puzzled as she felt. So she just went ahead and asked, even though she was very, very afraid of the answer.

"So, you are telling me you know where this David Buel is?"

Annie smiled and nodded. "He lives about a mile from here."

Julia felt stunned, more so than with any other bit of news that kept slamming at her in this case.

Stan was alive and if Annie was right, living just a mile from where they were sitting.

"Let's go arrest that bastard," Andor said, pushing his chair back.

"On what charge, Detective?" Annie asked. "You have no murder, you have adult children, he stole only a body twenty-two years ago, and he married five times without a divorce. I'm pretty sure the statute of limitations has passed on the theft. Not so sure about the bigamy charges. We'd have to talk with a prosecutor to figure out if being declared dead changes that."

Suddenly the four former detectives sitting around the table had nothing to say.

And all Julia could do was take slow, deep breaths, and try to make some sense out of all of this.

An impossible task.

CHAPTER TWENTY-SEVEN

October, 2014
Pleasant Hills
Las Vegas, Nevada

Lott sat alone at his kitchen table, working at a bowl of shredded wheat covered in milk, trying to get enough energy to just go to bed. In one day they had been in three states and discovered more about Stan Rocha and his life from twenty years ago than Lott ever wanted to know about another person.

A bunch of what they discovered wasn't pretty, right down to the point where the guy had stolen a body in Reno and faked his own death.

And by doing so left five wives and five children without a husband or a father.

He was some kind of creep, of that there was no doubt. A selfish, pathetic one as far as Lott was concerned.

One thing good had come of the day. The Cold Poker Gang

had cleared another cold case, one that Lott had given them no chance to clear when they started. That felt good.

The poker game this week was going to be fun.

And the Chief of Police was happy about it when Andor called him from the Bellagio.

Lott and Andor and Julia and Annie, along with the Chief of Police, had an appointment tomorrow morning at eleven to talk with the prosecuting attorney, Hanson Evans, about the possible charges against Rocha. Lott had a gut feeling there just wasn't going to be much Evans was going to be able to do.

Bigamy was a felony, but it was rarely prosecuted and now that Rocha was found alive, all the wives would have to do was file for an annulment or a divorce under Nevada law and the bigamy charges would be moot. And four of the wives hadn't even actually been legally married to Rocha, since he had first married Kate McDonald a few years earlier.

Plus the statute of limitations had passed on the body theft.

But there were still a few things that really nagged Lott about all this. And his tired mind just wouldn't let the worry go.

Lott had little doubt that Stan Rocha was devious enough to fake his own death. And enough of an ass to walk away from five wives and his kids. But he wouldn't have been able to do the actual theft alone. He had to have help, real money help, to do such a thing, and Rocha just didn't have the funds to do that.

And who could he have trusted to do such a thing and stay quiet for twenty-two years?

So who helped him? And why?

Suddenly the image of Kate McDonald being shocked about Stan's corporation flared into his memory. The governor's wife was actually very upset about that, more so than she should have been after all the years. She said she knew that Stan had been killed, so why be shocked at the corporation?

Was it possible that to clear out Stan from her life, maybe so she could get on with an affair with the future governor, Kate and the future governor had helped Stan fake his own death?

Having Stan suddenly die made sense for the future governor's wife. It solved the problem of her husband, the bigamist. It solved the problem of her moving on with her two kids, and having a regular relationship with someone her parents approved of.

And from the sounds of it, it also allowed Stan to just keep on with his search for lost treasures.

Lott got up and started pacing. Carol had hated it when he paced in the kitchen late at night, worrying about a case. But it helped him think.

He glanced at the clock over the stove. It was only a little before eleven in the evening. It felt more like three in the morning.

Annie would still be awake. More than likely this case was still bothering her as well.

A few seconds later Annie answered her cell phone. Lott could hear the sounds of a poker room in the background. More than likely she had joined a cash game at the Bellagio while waiting for Doc to get finished in the tournament.

"Sorry to bother you," he said.

She laughed. "Can't let this one go yet, huh Dad?"

"Exactly," he said. "Did your people do research into the governor and Stan's first wife?"

"They sure did," Annie said. "Hang on, let me get my bag from the desk here where I have all the files and then find a quieter place to talk."

He held on, still pacing the kitchen, as she asked for her bag, then ducked off to an area of the poker room with empty tables.

"Got it all right here," she said after a moment.

144

"When were Kate and the governor married?"

"Almost one year after Stan's fake death," she said. "You think she had a hand in helping him take the body?"

"I'm betting that she and the future governor both did," Lott said. "Only thing that makes sense. But I'm also betting, since she knew that Stan was still alive, she would have filed for divorce from Stan quietly at some point, just to get it on the record in case he suddenly came back to life or the actual identity of the body was discovered. Did you look for a divorce by Kate from Stan?"

"Shit," Annie said. "Of course she would have done exactly that. I'll get someone searching both Idaho and Nevada and we'll have the information before tomorrow morning."

Lott laughed. "We let that become public, we cause Kate and the governor no amount of political trouble."

"If they actually did help Stan fake his death," Annie said. "They deserve every problem that can be shoveled at them."

"Oh, I like your attitude, dear daughter," Lott said.

"So," Annie said, "is Julia there with you right now?"

"No, why?" Lott asked.

"Bummer," Annie said. "See you tomorrow morning."

Lott stopped pacing and hung up, staring at the phone for a moment. Sometimes his daughter just had a way of making herself very clear without actually saying anything on topic.

He took a deep breath and quickly dialed Rogers' number before he got cold feet.

She answered with a quick "Hi."

"Just wanted to say that it was great working and traveling and being with you today."

"Thank you," she said. "I wouldn't have managed to get through it all without you there."

"So get some sleep and I'll see you in the morning," Lott said.

"Thanks, I will," Julia said. "And thanks for the call. It made me smile."

"Night," he said.

"Night," she said in return.

And then he hung up.

He sat back down at the kitchen table to finish his now soggy shredded wheat.

That had felt right.

And she wasn't the only one smiling.

CHAPTER TWENTY-EIGHT

October, 2014
Café Bellagio
Las Vegas, Nevada

Lott was the only one in the Café Bellagio when Julia got there. Somehow he had again beaten her there after their meeting with the Prosecuting Attorney this morning. Andor should be right behind her somewhere. They all had their own cars.

She walked up to Lott, who smiled up at her from a table tucked against some plants to the right of the main door.

She went around to his side of the table and kissed him on the cheek, then sat down next to him.

She smiled at his shocked, but pleased look.

"That was for being such a nice guy and that wonderful phone call last night. I needed someone right at that moment to tell me they cared."

"I very much care," he said, looking her right in the eyes

with those fantastic, dark eyes of his. She couldn't imagine ever growing tired of looking into those eyes.

"I know," she said, keeping her gaze locked with his. "And I care as well. And once we get through this mess, I'd love to find out where this feeling between us might lead."

"Now that's a great plan, detective," he said, smiling.

Right at that moment all she wanted to do was lean over and kiss him completely. But out of the corner of her eye she could see Andor striding toward the table.

"Well, that meeting was a bust," Andor said as he grabbed a menu and dropped into a chair across from them. "We can't even arrest that bastard."

"We knew that going in," Lott said. "But we can cause a lot more grief than simply arresting him."

"Oh, oh, folks, Lott has that devious look on his face."

"I like it," Julia said, winking at him.

He kept smiling but blushed a little, which she found even more charming.

"Oh trust me," Andor said, "that look has gotten us into more trouble over the years than I want to think about."

"Not thinking of doing anything rash," Lott said. "Just this."

He pointed to where Annie was coming toward them with a young guy who looked to be in his late twenties. The guy had long brown hair, a short-sleeved blue dress shirt tucked into jeans, and he carried a backpack slung over one shoulder.

He was looking around as if he had never been in the place before.

Julia had no idea what Lott and Annie were up to, but after the surprise this morning about Kate McDonald getting a divorce from Stan after she knew he was supposedly dead, Julia had a hunch this punishment for Stan and Kate and the governor of Idaho was going to be pretty nasty.

And she liked that.

Since there wasn't a thing the prosecuting attorney could do that would be worth the state's time and money, revenge was just about the only card left to deal Stan and Kate and the governor for what they did to so many people.

Annie and her guest stopped at the table and Annie introduced the three of them, using the word detective in front of each of their names. Then she turned to the young man with her.

"Detectives, I'd like you to meet Robert Austin, the political reporter for the Idaho Statesman newspaper and a freelance journalist for the Associated Press."

Julia was stunned. And pleased beyond words.

Annie got herself and Robert seated, then said, "Doc sent his plane this morning to bring Robert here. I gave him all the information I had to read on the way down. Now it's up to you three to explain how all this came about and what you know."

"Over lunch, right?" Andor asked as a waitress approached.

"Over lunch," Annie said, laughing.

Julia reached over and touched Lott's arm. "Was this your idea?" she whispered.

"It was if you like it," he said. "Otherwise I'm blaming my daughter."

"I like it a lot," Julia said, laughing. "Far better than putting the bunch of them in jail."

And now, for the first time since she learned Stan was alive, she was looking forward to seeing his face. And the shock on it when he discovered that he and Kate and the governor's scheme was blown.

CHAPTER TWENTY-NINE

October, 2014
Café Bellagio
Las Vegas, Nevada

They spent an hour briefing the reporter on the story and all the poor kid did was get more and more excited. For a moment, Lott thought he just might start drooling.

"This story has everything," Austin said after they had filled him in on all the sordid details. "Politics, scandal with a sitting governor, bigamy, lost treasures, stolen bodies, and corporation underhandedness. This will hit the national nightly news, it's so strange."

"Perfect," Julia said.

"Can't thank you enough for calling me in," Austin said. "And that fantastic plane ride."

"Our pleasure," Annie said. "Just make sure every fact you publish is backed up, so this guy and the governor can't snake their way out of this."

"Oh, trust me," he said. "Both the AP and the Statesman check everything I do carefully. And I make sure it's accurate before I give it to them."

The kid sounded perfect to Lott. This case was going to make his career, of that there was no doubt. And from the looks of it, he already had a pretty good career.

"Have you got a lawyer looking into how much Rocha is going to owe each of his remaining four wives from his sale of the business?" Austin asked. "I'm pretty sure they should have gotten some of it under the laws of most states."

Lott sort of jerked and Julia sat beside him looking stunned. The question felt like it had almost quieted down the entire casino.

Lott couldn't believe he hadn't thought of that at all, and Julia suddenly seemed to lose focus in her eyes on just thinking about the idea.

"Hadn't even thought of that, huh?" Austin said, smiling, looking around at the stunned group of detectives. "And I am pretty sure that the IRS and Nevada State Tax Commission need to be informed on all this as well, since I'm betting there was a lot of hidden income over the years, fraudulently withheld from taxes."

"Oh, shit," Andor said. "This is getting better by the minute. Kid, I like you."

"Thanks, Detective," the kid said, smiling. "I'm sure I'll think of a few more nasty grenades to toss at this jerk before it's all over."

"Just keep lobbing, kid," Andor said, laughing. "Keep lobbing."

"And there's a lot of money there," Annie said. "All the property, water rights, mineral rights and such added up to millions and millions in the sale. I'll get our financial people on it, see what stones they can turn over."

"Thanks," Lott said.

"Yes, thanks," Julia said. And then she turned to Austin. "I'll give you any interview you want as long as you leave my daughter out of all this."

"Deal," Austin said. "I can't see bringing in the kids on this at all. So thank you, Detective."

At that point Andor picked up his cell phone and called the department. All of them watched as he nodded, then said, "We're on our way."

"What was that?" Annie asked.

Andor smiled. "The Chief of Police isn't happy we can't arrest this guy either, so he offered to put a car watching the house until we got there. Rocha is still inside. So what say we go jerk this guy's chain a little?"

Lott liked that idea a lot.

And beside him, Julia nodded and smiled. Then she said simply, "It will be my pleasure."

CHAPTER THIRTY

October, 2014
Near the University of Nevada Campus
Las Vegas, Nevada

Julia sat beside Lott in his Cadillac SUV and stared at the home tucked back under some trees in an older subdivision. Stan had ended up living a lot nicer than she and Jane had ever lived. And that made her angry as well.

Andor pulled in behind Lott and behind him Annie and the reporter arrived. Their plan was simple. Andor and Lott would go up to the door and introduce themselves. She would stay off to one side until the moment was right to step forward.

A television crew would be filming the entire thing from a hidden van across the street and a freelance photographer had joined Austin and would be taking pictures, for a time without Rocha even knowing about it.

Also, both Lott and Andor were wired for sound, so everyone in all the cars could hear the conversation.

"You ready for this?" Lott glanced over at her, clearly worried.

"If I hadn't discovered all the really shitty things this guy did to a lot of people, I wouldn't be. Now I'm just angry and want to bring him to justice, even if that justice is to take all his money and turn him over to the IRS."

"So that means you're ready?" Lott asked, smiling.

"I'm twenty-two years of ready," she said, smiling back at him.

With that they both stepped out into the warm afternoon air. It wasn't hot and a soft breeze blew the leaves in the trees.

"Nice place," Andor said, joining the two of them as they headed across the street.

"Better than any of the four wives he cheated got to live in," she said.

"Just don't shoot the bastard, Detective," Andor said. "Even though I doubt a jury in the world would convict you."

Julia laughed. "Oh trust me, we're not letting him off that easily."

The house was a two-story Tudor-style building with high-pitched roof and a front door that was up four steps off the sidewalk. The lawn was well-cared-for and very green, considering how hot the summer had been.

Julia stepped off to one side so when Rocha opened the door, he wouldn't see her.

Lott and Andor went up to the door and Lott turned to the cars across the street and signaled they should start.

Then Andor banged on the door.

A moment later Julia heard the door open and a man say, "Yes?"

"Detectives Lott and Williams," Andor said. "Are you David Buel?"

"I am," the man said, and that time the memory of Stan's voice came back strong.

"AKA Stan Rocha?" Lott said.

"Excuse me?" the man asked.

Julia stepped away from the side of the building and walked up the four steps until she was face-to-face with her husband. He had aged and his skin had weathered in twenty-two years. He now wore a moustache and beard. His hairline had receded and his hair had gone to salt and pepper. He had on brown slacks and a brown dress shirt and looked like any fifty-some-year-old executive home on a warm afternoon.

He looked at her puzzled for a moment until she said, "Hi, Stan. Nice seeing you so healthy after all these years of being dead."

He hesitated, his eyes growing wide as he recognized her. "Julia?"

"Detective Rogers to you," she said, her voice as cold as she could make it. "When you and your first wife and her boyfriend hatched the scheme to help you escape from your children and your mistakes, you lost all right to call me anything but Detective."

"So," Andor said, his voice low and mean, "We need you to step out of the house, sir, so we can talk with you."

Andor had his hand on his gun when he made that request, and Julia saw Stan swallow hard and nod.

Julia stepped down onto the sidewalk and Lott followed her.

Andor flanked Stan and they moved so that Stan was facing the television van and cameras.

"First off, Mr. Rocha, why did you fake your own death?" Andor asked.

Stan looked slightly panicked. "Kate wanted out and she

and McDonald were afraid that if I got caught with so many wives, it would look poorly on them."

"So you stole a body from Reno?" Lott said as Julia stood there, staring at her husband.

He kept glancing at her and then his eyes would dart away.

"No, I didn't take the body. Kate and McDonald did that in his van. It made me sick to have to help them dress the body in my clothes when they got down here."

Julia just shook her head at the excuse of a man she had married. The poor bastard had just cost the governor of Idaho his job.

"And when exactly did you find the lost Breyfogle Mine? And start the Breyfogle Corporation?" Lott asked, setting Stan up to lose all his money.

"Early 1989," Stan said, actually acting proud for a moment.

"And you didn't keep track of your other four wives?" Andor said. "Or any of your five kids?"

Stan shook his head and actually hung his head a little. "Kate said I didn't dare, being dead and all." Then he looked up, surprised. "Five?"

Julia didn't give him the courtesy of telling him about Jane. He didn't deserve to know. It would be up to Jane later on to decide if she wanted her father to know about her.

"So you left them for single mothers to raise?" Lott asked. "Most of your wives, you know, never heard about your fake death. They just thought you walked out on them."

"Oh," Stan said, his face going whiter than it had been before. "That's not what I wanted."

"And you left your mother and father wondering when you would come home," Andor said. "They didn't hear about your little scheme either."

Stan just shook his head, staring at the ground in front of him.

"Aren't you even a little bit sorry?" Julia asked, her voice far, far colder than she intended it to be.

"Every day," Stan said. "Four years after we staged my death, I told Kate I couldn't stand it anymore and wanted to see my children. But she said they would kill me if I ever opened my mouth or showed my face."

At that, Andor coughed, turning away slightly, trying to cover a laugh.

All Julia could do was shake her head.

"So did you find other lost treasures?" Lott asked.

Stan nodded, his face brightening again. "I did. And I'm still looking for the Lost Dutchman Mine."

"Well, I doubt you are going to be doing much of that from where you are going," Andor said.

Stan just looked puzzled.

Julia stared at the man she had let trick her for years. What had she ever seen in such a worthless piece of human trash?

Julia turned her back on her husband and waved for the reporter and camera crew in the van to come on over.

Stan's eyes got huge as he saw them come out of the van and another car.

"We expect you to answer every question they have for you honestly," Andor said, his hand back on his gun. He had moved between Stan and the door of his home. "I'll be right here making sure."

Lott and Julia started to walk away together when Stan called out to her. "Julia?"

She spun and walked back to him, getting right up into his face. "My name is Detective Rogers to you, asshole," she said, almost spitting at him. "And if you don't answer every question these reporters have for you completely and honestly, you will see me and my gun and my handcuffs once again and it won't be pleasant. Do you understand?"

Stan swallowed and then nodded.

"Do we have an agreement?" she demanded, inches from his face.

"Yes," he said softly.

"Yes what?" she shouted back at him.

"Yes, Detective," he said.

"That's better. Now make sure you answer everything truthfully. Trust me, you never want to see me again."

He nodded and she spun and strode back toward Lott.

Then she winked at him and she could tell that he barely got turned away from Stan before breaking into a smile and choking down the laughter.

Damned if that hadn't felt good. For the first time in a lot of years she felt free.

CHAPTER THIRTY-ONE

October, 2014
Near the University of Nevada Campus
Las Vegas, Nevada

They climbed back in the car and Julia looked over at the handsome man sitting beside her.

"Thank you," she said, smiling at him. She really had fallen for this man and she knew he had fallen for her. They both had a distance to go to get healthy and learn about each other, but she knew that would be part of the fun.

"I think that was all my pleasure," Lott said, giving her that grin she loved so much. "After all these years, it's great to put that case away for good."

"And that husband as well," she said.

Lott laughed at that and then asked, "So where next? Detective?"

She looked into his eyes and smiled. "I've got a daughter

who lives about five blocks from here. I think it's about time I tell her about her father, don't you?"

"Before she sees it on the news," Lott said, indicating the camera and reporter on the front lawn across the street.

"Yeah, better from me than that way. I'll give you the directions."

He glanced at her, a line of worry crossing his face. "You want me along?"

"Damn right I do," Julia said. "You two better get used to each other, since I plan on hanging around you for some time to come."

"I like the sounds of that," he said, breaking back into a wide smile and pulling the car away from the curb.

She reached over and rested her hand gently on his leg and said simply, "So do I, Detective. So do I."

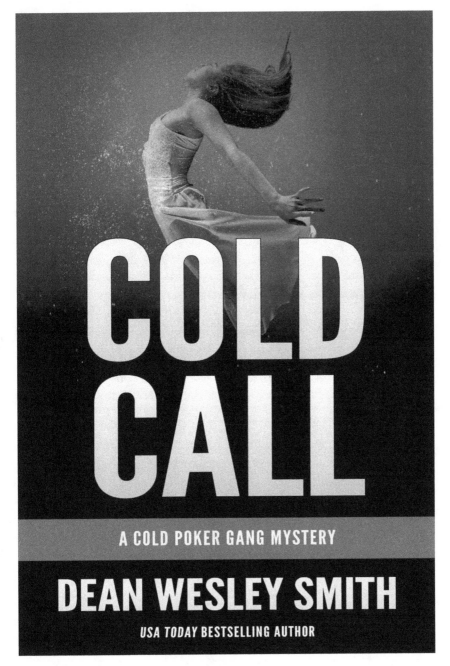

The Cold Poker Gang Mysteries continue with the next book in the series, Cold
Call. Following is a sample chapter from that book.

May 21, 2002
9:30 P.M.
Lake Mead, Outside of Las Vegas, Nevada

They'd come to the edge of the big lake to celebrate.

It was Danny and Carrie Coswell's first wedding anniversary, and since the night was so warm and both had just finished another long semester at UNLV, they had decided to go back to the place they used to go while dating.

It seemed right. Danny had loved the idea when Carrie suggested it over great steak dinners at the MGM Grand Hotel. They had gone home and changed clothes after the fancy dinner, changing back into their jeans and t-shirts and carrying sweatshirts in case the night cooled.

Danny loved how Carrie looked with her long blonde hair pulled back and her trim figure. Both of them ran for exercise and at times their class and study schedules allowed them to run together.

Danny really enjoyed being out at the lake, but Carrie liked it even more. She had told him that being along the vast expanse of Lake Mead made her feel part of the world. The silence and the wild of the shores of the lake were a sharp contrast to the constant motion and noise of Las Vegas.

He and Carrie were what some called childhood sweet-hearts. He knew he had loved her since the very first time he had seen her walking the halls of their high school, her books clutched against her chest, trying to find her locker. They had both been in the tenth grade and he offered to help her find her locker and they had became friends, then dated all the way through school after that.

They had wonderful memories of all the dances together, graduating together, and two years later getting married.

Below them, the lake was calm, its black surface spread out to the outlines of the hills on the other side. The faint moonlight shimmered across the water, making the night feel just a little brighter.

When dating, they would often go down the gentle gravel slope to the edge of the water, maybe even do some skinny dipping. But tonight they were content to sit on a blanket on the slight bluff, holding hands, leaning into each other, just talking about their first year of marriage, and their plans for the future.

Danny had called it their private place because they were tucked into what felt like a fort of brush and small scrub trees on the bluff. No one could see them, even down along the shore. And it was on a blanket in this private place that they had first made love in their senior year of high school.

The shelter in the brush with a view of the lake was a perfect place to dream about the future, and they had used it often to plan everything from their wedding to which classes to take.

Then a dark Mercedes eased slowly down the gravel road toward the edge of the lake, its lights off, its wheels making cracking noises on the rocks, its engine muffled by the tall, thick brush that lined the top of the bluffs along this part of the lake.

There was just enough moonlight to see the worn gravel road used during the day by fishermen and at night by kids like Danny and Carrie. Danny had parked their Toyota Camry in some brush about fifty paces back up the hill. It couldn't be seen at all from the gravel road.

The Mercedes was the wrong kind of car for a lake adventure. Danny could clearly hear the beautifully engineered chassis scrape against the rocks and bumps of the rough gravel and dirt road.

The only reason Danny could get his Camry this close to the lake was because he knew every bump and large dip. Clearly the Mercedes driver did not.

"What's a car like that doing on a road like this?" Danny whispered.

"I just want to know when he's going to leave," Carrie whispered back. She smiled at him. "I have plans for you, and I don't want an audience."

He laughed. Even after all the years, they still had a good time out here along the lake.

"He can't see us," Danny said. "More than likely just some rich daddy's kid on a date with his dad's car."

"Dad's not going to be happy if he notices the scrapes under the car," Carrie said, laughing softly.

The driver of the Mercedes stopped ten paces short of the edge of the bluff overlooking the water on the other side of the road.

Danny watched as a tall man got out. In the faint light from the Mercedes interior, Danny couldn't see the man's face, but Danny could see that the man had on a suit nearly as expensive as the car he drove.

"Not a date," Danny whispered.

Carrie grasped Danny's hand and said nothing as they watched.

The man opened the back door of his car and dug out a pair of dark coveralls. He pulled them on over his suit, put a dark hat on his head, and dark gloves on his hands.

With one final movement, he put on plastic boots over his shoes, the kind that golfers wear over their golf shoes on a rainy day.

Given that the night was perfect, not a sign of rain in sight, Danny had no idea what the man was up to with all the protective gear. But Danny's stomach was telling him it wasn't good.

Then, whistling a faint tune that seemed to just drift on the slight wind, the man moved around to the trunk of his car and opened it.

Since Danny and Carrie were just above the man and the trunk light came on, it was clear there was a human body in the trunk.

Carrie inhaled, about to scream, but Danny put a hand over her mouth before she could make a sound. He could feel her trembling beneath his touch.

Or more than likely, that was his own hand shaking.

With a swift motion, the man in the expensive suit and coveralls yanked a woman's body out of the trunk and slammed her to the ground on the rocks and gravel.

Danny wanted to be sick. Beside him, Carrie was grabbing his hand hard and trembling.

The rich guy pulled out the plastic sheet the woman had been on in the trunk, spread it out beside her, and then rolled her body onto the plastic like it was so much garbage.

The dead woman seemed young, with long blonde hair and nice clothes. She might have been pretty because she had a thin body, and she seemed very, very stiff. Nothing about her seemed to bend.

Danny still couldn't see the man clearly enough to pick him out of a crowd.

The man was whistling a little louder, clearly enjoying himself. The whistling sent chills through Danny's back. He knew they were witnessing pure evil.

The man pulled the woman and the tarp toward the edge of the bluff over the water. Then, with a strength that surprised

Danny, the man picked up the woman and tossed her into the water below.

The sound of her body splashing in the black lake water carried through the night air like a death knell.

"We've got to get out of here," Danny whispered to Carrie. "If he sees us, he'll kill us."

She nodded, still staring at the man on the edge of the bluff as he took a couple of rocks, wrapped the plastic around them, and then tossed the plastic into the lake as well.

"Wait," Carrie whispered. "Let's try to get the plate number. He hasn't noticed us so far. Maybe we're better off letting him leave first."

Danny nodded. He agreed with that now that he thought about it. They would not be able to be silent moving through the brush back to their car. They were in their hidden secret place. If they stayed still, the man wouldn't see them.

They waited and watched until the man took off his protective clothing, boots and all, wrapped rocks inside of them, and tossed the clothing in the water as well.

Then, still whistling, he climbed back into his car and shut the door.

The sound of the high-powered Mercedes engine cut through the night air. He quickly turned the car around in a wide area and went back up the road slowly, without lights or parking lights on.

It surprised Danny that a modern car could even move without at least some running lights on, but this car was nothing more than dark ghost moving along the narrow gravel road in the faint moonlight.

Danny thought his heart was going to pound right out of his chest. He was terrified the killer would see them, make them his next victims.

As the car headed slowly up the rough road, Danny eased out to see if he could read the license plate number.

Nothing but a faint dark outline of the car disappearing into the night.

When it vanished into the distance, Carrie let go of a long, shuddering breath, then burst into silent tears.

Danny let out a breath he didn't know he was holding and they both sat there, holding each other, shuddering.

Danny could see no evidence of what had just happened in the lake below.

He and Carrie had both been born and raised in Las Vegas. They heard about crime on the nightly news, but never had been this close to anything like this.

After a few minutes, Danny figured enough time had passed. He couldn't hear the Mercedes at all.

They moved as silently as they could to their car and then sat there for another few minutes.

Nothing moving in the dark night.

Danny finally started the car and faster than he had ever driven the gravel road, he headed for the main highway.

Within minutes, Danny and Carrie were speeding back into town along the old Boulder Highway, Danny driving as fast as he could do safely.

Next stop: the Las Vegas Police Department.

He just hoped they would get there alive.

NEWSLETTER SIGN-UP

Be the first to know!

Just sign up for the Dean Wesley Smith newsletter, and keep up with the latest news, releases and so much more—even the occasional giveaway.

So, what are you waiting for? To sign up go to deanwesleysmith.com.

But wait! There's more. Sign up for the WMG Publishing newsletter, too, and get the latest news and releases from all of the WMG authors and lines, including Kristine Kathryn Rusch, Kristine Grayson, Kris Nelscott, *Smith's Monthly, Pulphouse Fiction Magazine* and so much more.

To sign up go to wmgpublishing.com.

ABOUT THE AUTHOR

Considered one of the most prolific writers working in modern fiction, *USA Today* bestselling writer Dean Wesley Smith published almost two hundred novels in forty years, and hundreds and hundreds of short stories across many genres.

At the moment he produces novels in several major series, including the time travel Thunder Mountain novels set in the Old West, the galaxy-spanning Seeders Universe series, the urban fantasy Ghost of a Chance series, a superhero series starring Poker Boy, and a mystery series featuring the retired detectives of the Cold Poker Gang.

His monthly magazine, *Smith's Monthly*, which consists of only his own fiction, premiered in October 2013 and offers readers more than 70,000 words per issue, including a new and original novel every month.

During his career, Dean also wrote a couple dozen *Star Trek* novels, the only two original *Men in Black* novels, Spider-Man and X-Men novels, plus novels set in gaming and television worlds. Writing with his wife Kristine Kathryn Rusch under the name Kathryn Wesley, he wrote the novel for the NBC miniseries The Tenth Kingdom and other books for *Hallmark Hall of Fame* movies.

He wrote novels under dozens of pen names in the worlds of comic books and movies, including novelizations of almost a dozen films, from *The Final Fantasy* to *Steel* to *Rundown.*

Dean also worked as a fiction editor off and on, starting at Pulphouse Publishing, then at *VB Tech Journal*, then Pocket Books, and now at WMG Publishing, where he and Kristine Kathryn Rusch serve as series editors for the acclaimed *Fiction River* anthology series, which launched in 2013. In 2018, WMG Publishing Inc. launched the first issue of the reincarnated *Pulphouse Fiction Magazine*, with Dean reprising his role as editor.

For more information about Dean's books and ongoing projects, please visit his website at www.deanwesleysmith.com and sign up for his newsletter.